# Looking for Trouble

## A Blood Hounds Novel

Ron Schwab

Uplands Press

OMAHA, NEBRASKA

Uplands Press
1401 S 64th Avenue
Omaha, NE 68106
www.uplandspress.com

Publisher's Note: This is a work of fiction. Names, characters, places, and incidents are a product of the author's imagination. Locales and public names are sometimes used for atmospheric purposes. Any resemblance to actual people, living or dead, or to businesses, companies, events, institutions, or locales is completely coincidental.

Ordering Information:
Quantity sales. Special discounts are available on quantity purchases by corporations, associations, and others. For details, contact the "Special Sales Department" at the address above.

Uplands Press / Ron Schwab -- 1st ed.

ISBN 978-1-943421-50-3

# Looking for Trouble

A Blood Hounds Novel

# Chapter 1

A T AGE THIRTEEN, Trouble Yates was a budding capitalist. He had spent the afternoon selling weaned kittens to residents of the small town of Lockwood, Wyoming. Cats were selling at a premium these days. He could jingle five gold eagles in his pocket. Fifty dollars for five kittens. In the currently battered cattle market, a calf would not bring ten dollars, and he had three more litters in the barn that should put sixteen more kittens on the market in a few weeks. Cats were a gold mine in the fall of 1882 with rat overpopulation threatening to take over the country. The big cities had been sucking up any surplus felines. He had heard San Francisco businessmen were having cats brought in on ships and that folks would pay a hundred dollars for a good ratter on either coast.

Supply and demand. Some old Scot named Adam Smith wrote that. Mister Gaines, the banker, put a lot of store in this Smith. The banker always had "words of wisdom," the old guy called them, a lot of ideas about business that made sense to Trouble. But the banker had been around a spell and knew some things. Ma said that Matthew Gaines was forty-five years old, ten years older than her, ancient in his youthful eyes.

Cat populations had a way of growing, and sooner or later there would be a glut, Mister Gaines told him. When that happened, who would pay ten dollars for a kitten? Already, there were a few folks in town who had latched onto Trouble's idea and were raising cats. He had already figured out that competition would soon drive prices down. He should talk to Mister Gaines about how a person would go about shipping a load of cats to California. Or maybe send a bunch back east. Regardless, he was keeping his eyes open for other opportunities.

Fortunately, Trouble, whose baptized name was Brady, had stashed most of his money, whatever wasn't needed for food and other necessaries. Some of it was deposited in the Gaines Bank, but not all. Today's cat take would go in the tin box buried in the barn with the other gold pieces. He would dig up the box again, deposit the coins, put the box back in the hole and bury it, and then scatter cat poop over the top to hide his work. They had plenty of that around if a guy did not mind digging for it. He figured most would-be thieves would not look too hard under mounds of cat shit for anything valuable. Besides, Ma was the only one who had any notion there was money hidden in the barn. He had showed her where to find it.

He had not even told his best friend, Samantha Morris, who was his age and lived with her parents and two little brothers across the North Laramie River on the north side. The Morris home was no more than a quarter mile from the Yates place and an easy wade or stone hop across the shallow water that really did not earn a river designation in Trouble's mind. It generally was not much threat between spring thaws. During high water, a walker could usually make it over a crude footbridge that arched above the swift waters. He could not remember ever not knowing Sammy. She helped him sometimes with the cat herd and when Ma was ailing.

Sundown was still several hours distant, and he was no more than a half hour from home, as Trouble led his burro, Abner, along a well-traveled bumpy wagon trail that ran parallel to the river. The old burro never hurried and could be an obstinate critter, but Abner could pull a hefty cargo in the two-wheel cart that trailed behind him. The burro's load now consisted of an empty crate that had caged the kittens, Trouble's Winchester rifle, and a bulging possible bag that carried anything he figured might come in handy.

During the trek to Lockwood, a stack of the season's last melons had filled out the cart, which Trouble had dickered for sale to Jeb Oaks who operated Oaks General Store with his Brule Sioux wife, She Bear. Folks said Jeb had been born a slave, but somewhere along the trail he had picked up some business sense, because Trouble never felt he had got the best of the thirty-something Negro merchant in a deal. What he liked about Jeb, though, was that the man cut him no favors because he was a kid. Jeb dealt with him man to man, and he usually had learned a few things when he walked away from bartering with Jeb.

Trouble and his mother lived near the river on a 160-acre homesteaded farm that lay slightly less than two miles further west at the base of the Laramie mountain range that surrounded the lush valley of farms and ranches. Lockwood was a three-mile trip from the Yates farm. The town of some seven hundred people was a thriving commercial center and county seat of an area that included another eight hundred folks from the farm and ranch families that filled the valley. The population included nearly two hundred Brule Sioux who had established an off-reservation community of farmers, ranchers, and businesspeople. Thanks to funding of an organization called the "Lame Buffalo Association," the Sioux were quickly becoming successful entrepreneurs and blending into the populace, many intermarrying with their former enemies. Given the shortage of females in Wyoming Territory, the women especially had ample prospects to select from. Warriors had lost the luxury of multiple wives.

As he strode along the trail, tugging Abner, who was inclined to a more leisurely pace, Trouble pulled his battered low-crowned hat down on his forehead to block the glare of the sun's rays that seemed to be moving west ahead of him. The sun was fibbing about the day, he thought. A stiff wind was bringing a chill down from the mountains, and it was not as warm as it might appear from inside a house looking through window glass. He was grateful now for the sheepskin coat Ma had insisted he take with him. Of course, he would have taken it anyway, but he had learned that it pleasured his mother to remind him of such things.

With the prospect of colder weather coming on, Trouble's mind turned to business. He would need to start cutting and selling firewood again soon. He had a healthy supply of oak, ash, and hickory already cut to fireplace size and ready for marketing. The inventory had come from last year's cutting, left to season for better burning. The quarter section had almost forty acres of forested ground, consisting mostly of good hardwoods, including some walnut trees that he was saving for sale to craftsmen someday. It had occurred to him that most folks had more trees than they wanted on their properties. They wanted the ground cleared for farming and grazing. A few more years, and he might start up a sawmill, even buy old Taylor Brown's operation. The grumpy old fart didn't get his work out and would probably sell cheap by then. Lease up woodlands for a little or nothing, clear the land, and turn the good stuff into lumber and the leftovers into firewood. No waste.

Trouble's dreams were suddenly interrupted by the sound of a woman's hysterical screaming followed by the cracks of gunfire. He yanked Abner to a stop, which wasn't much of a trick, since he was more interested in chewing the trailside grass than heading home. He snatched up the rifle, reached in the possible bag, grabbed some extra cartridges and stuffed them in the pocket of his faded denims. Then, he raced in the direction of the tumult. The screaming was coming from Lucy Brisbane's house, the three room, clapboard cottage she rented from the Double R ranch owned by lawyer Ethan Ramsey and his wife. The place was some hundred yards off the trail and hidden by forested acres normally accessed by a wagon trail that connected to a road located on the opposite side of the farmstead.

Trouble weaved stealthily through the trees, and by the time he approached the house, the screaming and gunfire had stopped, but he could hear the murmur of voices and the whinnying of nervous horses. He crept nearer to view the scene, and as he moved in and crouched behind the undergrowth, he tried to make sense of what was happening. Then he saw the bullet-riddled and bleeding body of the sturdy, white-haired, mustachioed man lying face up in front of the little railed porch, hat and pistol on the ground nearby. Four men looked down at him, two standing with pistols in their hands, the other two mounted. The wounded man moved, arm flopping helplessly as he tried to reach his gun, and a tall, black-bearded man and another shorter, paunchy man fired more shots into the body.

Sheriff Will Bridges. He recognized the sheriff's gray gelding tied to the hitching post in front of the house. The four men waited, one of the riders clutching the reins of two extra horses. A fifth man stepped out of the open doorway, a slim, swarthy man, half-breed or Mexican maybe, with a broad grin. Dressed in black like

a gunslinger looked in a Ned Buntine or Prentiss Ingra-
ham dime novel. He carried his gun low on the hip, too.

The man spoke with an indefinable accent. "Lucy's
had her last poke, boys. She won't be talking none."

"Well, we shut Bridges up," said one of the riders attired in a business suit, who looked familiar, but whose
name Trouble could not come up with. He handed the
reins of a black gelding he had been holding to the man
in black. He recognized Ferd Bullock, the sheriff's longtime deputy, who clutched the reins of two other nervous
mounts. But what was Bullock doing just sitting calmly
in his saddle? He should be arresting these outlaws.

Trouble instantly realized that the deputy had to be
a part of whatever had taken place here. He could not
go to the law about this. Still on his hands and knees, he
started to back away slowly when a twig snapped, and the
black clad man looked his way. He froze and waited.

"Somebody's out there. I can smell him," the gunslinger said, drawing his pistol and stepping in Trouble's
direction. Trouble leaped up, turned, crouched low, and
raced through the brush and trees.

He heard Bullock yell, "That's Trouble Yates. Kill the
little bastard. Kill him, or we all hang."

Two gunshots cracked as Trouble weaved through the
trees, but the shooter was guessing, because as near as he

could tell the shots were not even close. The timber was thick here, and he could outrun any horse in the tangle of brush and trees. And he was wearing his clodhoppers in contrast to the riding boots worn by his pursuers. They could not run him down in a sprint afoot. There were a few more wild shots, and he could hear the men screaming profanely at each other. Brush and tree limbs cracked and snapped behind him as someone struggled to crash a horse through nature's barrier.

When he reached the trail, he snatched his possible bag from the cart, untied Abner's lead rope and slapped the burro on its rump to head the critter towards home. He knew Abner would get there on its own when the burro decided it was time for grain. The burro tossed its head and looked at Trouble and then returned to grazing.

He could hear a man on horseback nearing, so he slid down the riverbank and stepped into the shallow water near the edge. Trouble knew every inch of the North Laramie River and ran upstream over the mix of gravel and river rock that covered the stream bed, hoping the clear, racing water would erase any sign of his passage. When he reached the scattering of flat rocks that stretched across the river before the water abruptly dropped several feet, he hopscotched over the stones to the other side.

He rushed up the gently sloping bank and disappeared into the woods.

He felt his chest heaving as he ran through the thick undergrowth and the cottonwood and aspen trees that to his benefit needed serious thinning. He worked his way up a knoll and dropped to the ground when he reached the top. He flattened his body against the earth and looked back southeast where he had abandoned Abner and the cart. The tall, black-bearded gunman stood behind the cart, clutching the reins of a sorrel gelding, his head moving from side to side as he searched the trail and river for some sign of Trouble Yates. Abner, evidently annoyed by the appearance of a newcomer, stopped grazing and started up the trail at a slow pace. The animal would lead the killers to his mother's house. Of course, Ferd Bullock, the deputy sheriff, would know the location anyhow.

He worried about Ma. Would they harm her? She knew nothing about what Trouble had seen, but would they believe her? But if they caught him there, the sheriff's killers would be forced to kill them both. No, he had to stay away from the place until he figured out what to do. Sammy. He had to talk to Sammy before he took off.

# Chapter 2

TROUBLE WAS LUCKY. Sammy Morris was milking the old Jersey cow when he walked into the farmyard. He peeked through the barn door and watched her for a bit. She might pass for a boy from the backside, slim as she was, and dressed in clodhoppers, baggy, denim britches and one of her father's flannel shirts that nearly swallowed her. But the long sable hair, pulled back in a ponytail that dropped to midback suggested there might be a female sitting perfectly balanced on that one-legged milking stool—he needed a three legger or he would end up on his butt more often than not.

Just this past summer, Trouble had started to think of Sammy as female. Early on, when they were swimming naked in their favorite waterhole formed by a sharp cut in the river's course, she had apparently noticed him staring at the nubs that had seemed to overnight appear on her chest and turned away. And, despite the icy water, he had felt his pizzle swell and stiffen, fortunately hidden by the water below his waist. Nothing was said between them, but after that they both stopped shucking their clothes to bare skin when they swam. Underthings covered their respective male and female parts, but when the garments were soaked with water, there was not much left to the imagination. They remained best friends, but Trouble sensed that changes were coming on.

He stepped into the barn and spoke, "Sammy, we've got to talk."

Samantha almost tumbled off the milking stool at the sound of his voice but recaptured her balance and stood to face him, her dark eyes smoldering with anger. "Brady, why did you sneak up like that? I almost peed my britches."

Darn, she was a pretty thing, he thought. He had not looked at her that way six months back. Her olive-tinted skin, the heritage of her half-blood Sioux mother, glowed in the slivers of sunlight that crept through the unlatched and open barn window. And now it bothered him more than a little that with long-legged Sammy stretching to five feet and eight inches tall, he could only reach her height on his tiptoes. He had enjoyed a good growth spurt lately, though, and Ma had reminded him that there was plenty of time for a growing boy, not so much for most girls. "Sorry," he said. "Your folks around?"

"No. They went to town for a week's supplies. Pop always takes Mom to 'The Chowdown' for supper before they head home. Won't be back till after dark. But I don't have time to jabber long. I've got to finish milking Rosie, and then I've got to fix supper for the boys. They're fishing down by the river. What are you doing here, anyway? I thought you were selling kittens today."

"I did. But something happened, and I'm on the run. Can't go home. And you ain't seen me. Understand?"

"*Haven't* seen you. I swear, when you bother to show up for school, you read and cipher better than anybody. You need to speak right," she scolded. "Now what is this all about? Did you kill somebody or something?"

"No. But I saw somebody that was killed. And the killers caught sight of me. That's all I'm saying. It ain't safe for you to know more. I'm hiding out till I figure out what to do. They're looking for me, and I'm heading into the mountains."

"Oh, Brady. You've got to go to the sheriff."

"Can't. And don't anybody go to the deputy. I want you to tell Ma that. Can you help her some with the cats and the chores till I get back? Maybe Levi would help out, too.

Tell him I'll pay him good when I next see him. Shouldn't be gone more than a couple days."

"This sounds really dumb, Brady. There's got to be somebody you can go to for help."

"Mister Gaines, maybe. But they'll be watching the town. There were five men where I saw this, but there could be more. There's something fishy going on."

Samantha said, "I can hide you here in the barn."

"And risk the lives of you and your family? Besides, they would be searching places like this. No, I'm heading out now. Remember, you ain't seen me."

"Wait." She raced to the back of the barn and returned shortly with a rolled-up buffalo robe bound with rope. "Pop keeps this around for strangers that drop by for a meal and a place to stay for the night. You will need something if you're going to higher ground. It was grandpa's, so it's seen better days, but it's better than nothing."

It was an ugly flea-bitten thing, Trouble thought. But Sammy was right. It would be dangerous to go into the high country without something to help ward off the cold at night, especially if he could not have a fire because of fear of detection. His sheepskin coat would not be enough to keep him warm at night. Sammy helped him slip his arms through the rope loops she had apparently made for backpacking. The load felt awkward at first but was not a terrible burden. Leave it to Sammy to think of such things.

"I've got to get moving," Trouble said.

"Do you have anything to eat?"

"No. I'll hunt game, catch some fish."

"Have you got lucifers to start a fire?"

"Yes, if I decide it's safe to build one. You are starting to sound like Ma."

She ignored his jibe. "And, if it's not, you will eat raw fish?"

"If I got to. And there should be cattails aplenty yet about the lakes and ponds. I love the roots. There's more to eat out there than you'd think if you know what you're looking for."

Samantha said, "Wait a minute."

She disappeared out the barn door, and he watched her run toward the log house, constructed in the shape of a "T" because of wings added to the structure since it was built a dozen years earlier. Sammy could run fast as a jackrabbit. He had not challenged her to a race for several years because he was weary of defeats inflicted by a girl. Sammy had never made fun of him, though, always a gracious winner.

She had always made him feel special, refusing to adopt the nickname first endowed by old Missus Traum.

She was one of the teachers at the Lockwood school who saw him riding his paint gelding toward the schoolhouse one morning and was overheard by several students when she said, "Here comes trouble." Butch Hugel, an obnoxious, thirteen-year-old bully, whom ten-year-old Brady Yates had whipped the day before, heard the remark and started calling him "Trouble," even after the smaller Brady bloodied the older, bigger boy's nose again. Others took up the name, and soon Brady had accepted the new moniker, deciding that was an improvement over "Runt," the name Butch had taunted him with for most of their school days. Sammy had chided him often about his quick temper and tendency to take offense, and the new name had seemed to cut the frequency of provocation, or he had taken better control over his anger. He was never certain which. Regardless, as he turned his attention to commercial endeavors, he had found he had less inclination to fuss and fight.

Samantha returned from the house carrying a cloth bag bulging at its seams. She said, "Your hands are full with your rifle and possible bag. Let me tie this to your belt. I'll use a slip knot, so a tug on the end will release it. Just some leftover biscuits and cookies, but it will fill your belly for a few meals—well, maybe just one the way you eat."

She hitched the rawhide drawstring to his belt and stepped back and looked at him as if she were judging a horse. But tears glistened Sammy's eyes, and her perusal made him uneasy. "I'd better git," he said.

Samantha stepped forward and embraced him and planted a soft, quick kiss on his cheek before releasing him. "You take care, Brady Yates. I'll look after your ma and take care of chores at your place. But if you're not back soon, I am taking things into my own hands."

Trouble could feel her kiss burning a hole in his cheek, and he turned away, jogged across the yard, and disappeared into the trees.

# Chapter 3

THE HAZE OF dusk was coming on, and Samantha and her brothers had just finished supper when the shepherd cow dog commenced barking in the farmyard. Ned did not bark when family or Brady came onto the place, so she knew her parents were not returning home. She stood up and peered out the window. A rider dressed in black, astride a black horse. He did not have the look of a wrangler seeking out work.

"Levi, Jake. Go to your bedroom. Stay put till I tell you to come out."

"I wanna go fish some more," seven-year-old Jacob protested.

"Mom and Pop put me in charge. If you don't want the razor strap when they get home, you'll do what I say."

Levi took his brother's hand and led him away. Samantha hurried to the gunrack above the door, reached up and pulled down the Henry rifle, quickly checking to confirm it was filled with cartridges and levering one into the chamber. She leaned the rifle against the wall just inside the doorway, reminding herself to keep the rifle nearer than the visitor.

Her heart raced as she opened the door and stepped out onto the covered veranda, taking care not to move too far from the doorway. The rider dismounted, and led his horse toward the porch railing, and she took several steps back. He stopped.

"Nothing to worry about, little lady," the man said with a voice that seemed too deep for such a slight man. "My name's 'Slick.' I mean no harm."

She remained silent, acutely aware of his eyes studying her.

"I'm looking for somebody. Afraid he might be laying hurt someplace. My friend found his burro and empty cart."

"Who is your friend?" she asked.

"Let me talk to your pa."

"My father and mother are picking late corn on the east acres. They will be along soon." She could tell he did not quite swallow her lie, but he wasn't sure, either.

"I don't suppose I could come in and have a cup of coffee and a biscuit or a slice of bread? Ain't had a bite to eat since morning. Or maybe you would bring me out something?"

"Stay put. I'll bring you out something." She walked back into the house and picked up the rifle before she returned to the veranda with the weapon leveled at the stranger's chest. "I know how to use this. If you've got anything to say, speak up. Otherwise, get out."

She had her finger pressed against the trigger, her eyes on his hands. One move, and she would drop him.

Slick was appraising her and apparently understood his position. He said, "You're a saucy gal, ain't you? That's how I like them. A bit of sauce on the meat makes it tastier. Okay. I'm looking for a boy named Trouble Yates."

"I know him. Our families are longtime neighbors. If he had shown up hurt, I would have got help for him."

"You hiding him out here?"

"What would he be hiding out from? All I know about Trouble is that he told my father he couldn't help with corn picking because he was taking cats to town today. That's why my mother's helping pick corn."

"Can I take a look around in your barn?"

"If you are worried about Trouble Yates being hurt, it doesn't make sense you would be looking for him in our barn, but help yourself." She raised the rifle and fired a shot in the air before levering another cartridge and returning aim to Slick's chest. "Go ahead and look in the barn."

"What was that shot all about?"

"Signal to my folks. They will be here soon. My father has got the shotgun and my mother has a Winchester. Maybe you can take us all down, but you will be calling an army of law this way if you do. And for what? Looking for some kid that sells cats?"

Slick's eyes narrowed, and he sent her a glare that spat hate. "We'll meet up again, young lady. That's a promise." He wheeled his big gelding around and rode away at a gallop.

Samantha did not leave the veranda until the rider was out of sight. Then she went inside and sat down on a chair at the kitchen table. Her right hand still clutched the rifle as she commenced trembling uncontrollably. Would she have shot the man? Unquestionably. And she would not have missed. She could handle any kind of long gun with accuracy. Not as good as Brady. They hunted together all the time. She might outrun him in a race, but she doubted anybody in the county was better than Brady with a rifle. She should have pulled the shotgun off the rack today, though, in hindsight. More intimidating up close, and shaky hands wouldn't have thrown off aim. She would remember that.

Now, what to do? Her first instinct was to race across the river and warn Sarah Yates, maybe bring her back to the house some way. On second thought, however, she decided Sarah might have already had callers, or would have before Samantha could get there. And if Sarah were to talk to somebody looking for Brady, it was better if she knew nothing. Her surprise and ignorance would be genuine. Also, if searchers were after Brady, they would only draw more attention if they went on a killing spree. Sarah was not likely in danger, not yet anyway. She would wait till her parents were home. She had to tell them what little she knew and about the visit from the scary stranger. Dad would go with her to check on Sarah Yates.

# Chapter 4

S ARAH YATES WAS besieged by near panic when Abner and the cart showed up in the yard without Brady. She could not imagine her son abandoning the burro except in the direst emergency or accident. She had been sitting at the kitchen table staring out the window and enjoying the absence of the spells of double vision that had been plaguing her the past few months. It had been a good day till now. With the help of her cane, she had found the strength with only a single rest break to slice ham for bean soup and bake some biscuits and ginger cookies. Brady, more often than not, had to help her with meals, or, on the worst days, do the cooking himself, always without complaint.

The meal was prepared for Brady's arrival, but surely he would appear soon, and she would be more than glad to warm things up. Dear God, just bring that special boy home safe. He was her life, the inspiration that got her out of bed each day.

It occurred to Sarah that the burro could not remain hitched to the cart all night, and the sun was already slipping behind the mountains that were casting eerie shadows over the valley. She needed to unhitch Abner from the cart. It was grain time, so he would probably follow her to his stall in the barn.

Cane in one hand and resting the other on the table, she lifted herself to her feet. A moment of dizzying weakness, and she began her cautious, deliberate steps to the door. Once on the porch, she shuffled to the sturdy cedar handrail fashioned by her craftsman neighbor, Caleb Morris, a half dozen years back, shortly after her balance and weakness problems came on. She walked snaillike out to the cart where Abner waited, eyeing her curiously.

She had just reached the cart when she saw a rider veering off the river trail and heading in her direction. A bearer of bad news? The tremors started in her fingers as they were wont to do when she was tense or stressed. She did not recognize the black-bearded man who approached her on a sorrel gelding. She scolded herself for not having her derringer secreted in the waist pouch fashioned for that purpose on her dress. Of course, her hand would have been too shaky to hold it, much less aim the gun, but she would not flinch at the notion of killing a man. She had learned that the night she gave her husband a boost on his way to hell.

Blackbeard wore a plainsman hat and did not appear too menacing despite his bearlike form. He displayed a congenial smile, but she could not make out his eyes. She trusted eyes more than lips in taking the measure of strangers. He reined in his mount a respectable distance from her, taking care not to crowd her, she figured.

"May I step down, ma'am?" he asked, his voice surprisingly soft and mellow.

"You may. But don't keep me waiting. I know you have bad news. Tell me. Now. Please."

He dismounted and took a few steps toward her and stopped, leaving a good twenty feet between them. "Ma'am, why do you think I've got bad news?"

"My son, Brady. His cart and donkey showed up without him. Something terrible has happened to him. I just know it."

"Ma'am. I just made a river crossing. I was told I could catch this trail and go direct to Lockwood. Hoping to find work there. Don't know nothing about your boy. What's his name?"

"Brady. But he's got a nickname. Lots of folks call him 'Trouble.'"

The man chuckled. "That's some name, but I've been called worse in my day. My handle is James Tolliver. Might I be asking yours?"

"Sarah. Sarah Yates."

"Yates. I rode with a man named Yates from up this way some years back. Al Yates. Any relation?"

She leaned against the wagon, as a wave of weakness swept over her. She was silent a few moments, pondering whether to admit her kinship. Then she blurted out, "Alfred Yates was my late husband. He disappeared a dozen years ago. Six years back the judge declared him dead."

Tolliver said, "That's about the time I lost track of him. If he's alive, you're better off if he ain't here. Now, about your boy, maybe I can be on the lookout for him. When was the last you seen him?"

"This morning. He took Abner and merchandise to town to sell. He was past due home and then Abner shows up with the cart."

"I noticed you've got a hard time getting about, ma'am. Why don't you let me put Abner up and unhitch him from the cart? Then I'll be on my way."

"Oh, I'd be so thankful if you would do that. Then come up to the house. I've got a meal ready, and Brady's not here to eat it. The least I can do is feed you. My thanks for the chores and not bringing bad news."

"I'd take that kindly, ma'am. I ain't had a homecooked meal in a long spell. Mind if I give my horse a bit of grain and hay while I'm here? I'd gladly pay."

"No. Take care of your horse. There is a grain bin at the back of the barn. Abner's stall is next to it. We have two mules, a paint horse and dry milk cow in the pasture east of the barn. Brady grained them this morning and the grass is plentiful, so they should be fine till morning. Thankfully, I don't have a cow to milk. Dollie's huge with calf and won't freshen for a month yet."

Tolliver grasped the burro's halter and led Abner and his horse toward the barn. Sarah called after him, "Don't mind the cats. They're Brady's business. Most are probably out hunting right now."

She slowly made her way back to the house, feeling a surge of energy with company coming for supper. Back in the house, she stepped into her bedroom to check herself in the mirror. A few loose ends in her chestnut-colored hair, but she could not do much without untying the ribbon that held her pulled back, shoulder length mane in place, and her hands were not steady enough to do that. Thankfully, Sammy had trimmed her hair and helped with washing it only a few days earlier. She straightened her pale, yellow blouse and full cotton skirt and went to the kitchen to warm up the meal on the woodstove.

When Tolliver came to the house after caring for the animals, she invited him to sit down at the kitchen table. She noticed him watching her as she dipped ham and beans into his bowl and placed a plate of hot biscuits on the table. She had not been alone with a mature man at her table for years, a strange feeling but not unpleasant. She wondered if he found her ugly. She had once been thought a pretty woman, and Brady and Samantha assured her that at age thirty-five she still was. But the mysterious disease had eaten away much of her flesh it seemed, and she was aware that she might be thought a skinny woman absent the womanly curves she once took pride in.

She sat down across the table from him. "Honey or apple butter," she said, "and I have plenty more biscuits, so eat your fill. I will have coffee ready shortly. I hope you drink coffee."

"Got to have coffee with my biscuits, and I will eat my fill. I ain't had a bite since morning and that weren't nothing to brag about. I can't thank you enough for your hospitality, especially when you're worried about your boy. Where do you think he might have went?"

"That's what worries me. I have no idea, and it's not like him to be late. He's got a clock in his head. Always on time, even with all the projects he is working at. He stops to eat, and maybe he will sleep four or five hours, and then he's out working at something. Thinks he's got to support us. And we do live better because of all his "businesses," as he calls them, but we wouldn't starve. I own a quarter section, and we could almost get by off the rents."

Tolliver seemed to savor the soup and biscuits, and Sarah enjoyed watching him eat. He was a big, solid man, mostly muscle she realized now that she saw him up close, no rolls of fat lopping over his belt. She would like to see the face under the beard, but his brown eyes seemed kind and gentle. He had the odor of sweat and horse one would expect of a man who had spent some days on the trail, but she found it alluring rather than repulsive. How long since she had been with a man? She estimated nearly fourteen years if only voluntary fornication counted.

"Ma'am," Tolliver asked, "ain't none of my business, but how did you come to be at this place?"

"Well, Mister Tolliver . . ."

"Please, call me James."

"If you will call me Sarah. I met Alfred Yates in Kansas City right after I finished high school and the war was winding down."

"An educated woman."

"In books, perhaps. But not in the ways of life. I was seventeen when Alfred Yates came into the tailor shop where I worked and employed me to make him a new suit. He claimed to be a discharged Union Army captain. To keep it short, he swept me off my feet, and two months later we were married and on our way to Wyoming Territory, a good place for a deserting private to get lost, I learned later. We homesteaded this place under my name, obviously to keep his name off the public record, but fortunately as it turned out."

"I can't believe it. Al farmed?"

"We settled on the farm. Some friendly neighbors helped with a dugout. It wasn't much, but I had hope. Alfred wasn't cut out to be a farmer or anything that worked. I found a job with a tailor in town—it was a part of his general store—and I took up dressmaking in addition to creating men's suits and garments. I helped build a thriving business, and he turned it over to me, as Lockwood grew and he didn't have time to handle it. I even bought a small building for my own shop. Alfred would leave for weeks at a time—looking for a gold strike, he said—and I hired men to help me keep the farm going. I helped with the planting and livestock care, when I wasn't working in town, and I did well enough. Then after Brady came along, Alfred left for good."

"But you stayed on."

"I love this valley and the mountains that surround us, and I know Brady does, too. And I had the tailor and dressmaking shop in town. I made a nice living until the illness came along and disabled my fingers for stitching and sewing. I hated giving it up, but I had saved some money back and had the farm rents, so, if I was careful with the spending, we could eke by. And then Brady started earning money. Before his tenth birthday, he was latching onto odd jobs. Then he started cutting firewood and selling it. Two years ago, a tomcat showed up here, and then a few female stragglers. He kept them fed and made straw piles in the barn for cold winters. A few litters, and he started selling kittens in town for ratters. He collected more females, traded with some folks, because he figured that like livestock, a tom shouldn't be mating with his own daughters." She felt scarlet spread across her face at her mention of a tom's breeding protocol.

"It sounds like Brady and his mother are a mighty resourceful pair. And it's clear where Brady learned his work habit. I can't help but admire you, Sarah. But you don't seem sick when we're talking here like this. You're just a pretty lady telling me interesting stories about your life. I hope I'm not speaking out of turn."

She blushed again but admitted to herself that his words were more welcome than he could ever know. "My illness comes and goes. There is not a name for it, I guess, and not much known about the ailment. Doctor Weintraub in Lockwood is a fine physician and has read everything he can find about the symptoms. It hits people in the prime of life and the symptoms strike in waves, blurred vision, muscle weakness, the shaking and tremors, extreme fatigue. There are others. Strange thing is that most can live a long time with it, maybe a normal life span. Something else is likely to kill you before this does. Some folks will have the symptoms disappear for months or years. I went three months once and thought I was cured before the illness suddenly came back."

"I'm sorry. It must make things hard for you."

"I'm just grateful I have a good chance of seeing my boy grown to manhood. Folks have to face a lot worse." Her words reminded her of Brady's absence. This man had distracted her from the fate of the most important person in her life. "I need to do something about finding out about Brady. Where he is. What's happened to him."

"What does Brady look like?"

"Blond hair, like wheat straw. Eyes blue as the mountain sky on a clear day. He's thirteen but on the small side, not yet five and a half feet tall."

"I'll keep an eye out. When I get to town," Tolliver said, "I'll ask around, notify the sheriff he is missing. Please don't worry too much. He sounds like a young man who can take care of himself. What if someone was looking for him and he didn't want to be found, where would he go?"

"That's easy. The mountains. If he can get away from work, that's where he heads. He reads about the old mountain men, talks to a few of the old timers when he is in town. He has even done some trapping along the streams higher up and sold a fair number of pelts. He says the market's not what it was in the old days, but it can still be profitable if you know where to set the traps. And, he doesn't say so, but it gives him and excuse to go into the mountains."

They talked for the better part of an hour before Sarah realized she had learned virtually nothing about this stranger. He had a knack for coaxing talk out of a person, pulling out words that might be regretted later. She decided it was time for her to learn something about the questioner. Then there was a rapping at her door.

Tolliver leaped from his chair, and she saw his fingers move to the butt of the pistol holstered at his waist. He moved off to the side of the door. "Answer," he said softly.

She remained seated and called, "Who is it?"

A man's voice answered. "It's Caleb Morris, Sarah. Sammy's with me."

She didn't want them to be surprised by her guest, and Tolliver had not pulled his pistol from his holster. "I have company. Come in."

The door eased open, and Caleb, a tall, lean man with a sunburned face and straw hat pulled low on his forehead, stepped in. He looked at Tolliver and apparently sensed no immediate threat, so he spoke to his daughter who was obviously standing some distance back from the door opening. "Come on up, Sammy."

Samantha entered the house carrying a bag. "We came with the eggs you needed," Samantha said, "and I baked some cookies I thought you and Brady might enjoy." She looked around the long room that had the kitchen space at one end and transitioned to a parlor at the other. "Is Brady in the barn? I wanted to ask how his cat sales went."

"No, he's late getting home. I'll tell you about it later. First, I would like you to meet Mister Tolliver. He was passing this way and helped me with some chores, so I invited him for supper. James Tolliver, these are my neighbors, Caleb Morris and his daughter, Samantha."

Tolliver stepped forward and extended his hand, and Caleb received it and tendered a warm smile.

"Pleased to meet you, James. You headed for Lockwood?"

"I am. Looking for work. Maybe as a top hand in a ranch operation. I know the cattle business."

"With winter coming on," Caleb said, "it's a bad time to be looking for cow work. Most ranches are laying off instead of hiring, but I wish you well."

"Won't get a job if I don't look. I'd best be on my way. Won't need supper but got to find a room."

"Lockwood Hotel on Main Street has rooms. Clean enough. Not much bug trouble. And a pair of Brady's cats keep it free of mice and rats," Caleb said. "I would take it slow on the trail in the dark. Lot of pits and ruts. Forty-five minutes will get you there easy."

"Thanks for the advice." Tolliver turned to Sarah. "I thank you for the fine meal, ma'am. I know you are worried, but I'm sure your son will return soon. I'll be asking about. It has truly been a pleasure meeting you." He plucked his hat from the wall peg near the door and disappeared into the darkness.

Something strange was going on here, Sarah thought. She narrowed her eyes and looked at Caleb Morris and Samantha. "Sit down here at the table where I've got the lantern turned up, you two. You brought me the eggs yesterday—and more cookies than we can eat in two weeks."

Caleb said, "There is a man on the knoll overlooking the house. I saw the flash of light when he lit a cigarette after we crossed the river. He's watching this place."

"Watching my house? Why on earth would anybody do that?"

"They are looking for your son."

"Brady? Abner and the cart came home without him. Why are they looking for him?"

"Don't excite yourself, Sarah. We have reason to think Brady's fine—for now anyhow. Let me tell my part of the story, and Sammy can tell the rest."

"Caleb, please, tell me what is going on."

"Well, Millie and me was in town a big part of the day, and just as we was leaving The Chowdown after supper, there was a big hullabaloo over by the sheriff's office. Deputy Bullock was out front talking to a couple of Circle D cowhands. Some men from the saloons was gathering up there, too. I left Millie at the buckboard with the team and went over to see what had got everybody so worked up. Well, it turns out somebody killed Sheriff Bridges and Lucy Brisbane over at her place. The cowhands had gone over to . . . uh . . . visit Lucy and found the sheriff out front torn up with bullets and Lucy in the house shot twice in the head—and I don't think I need to say more."

Sarah knew that Lucy earned her living as a prostitute out of her own home, thereby avoiding the sharing of at least half her fees with the owner of a bordello. She was not comfortable discussing such things with Brady, but he had commented once that Lucy Brisbane was a smart businesswoman. "Cut out the middleman when you can," he had said. She had quickly changed the subject.

"I fail to see what this has to do with Brady."

Caleb said, "Sammy, you tell the rest."

Samantha told Sarah about Brady's visit to the Morris farm and the likelihood he was being pursued. "I said I wouldn't wait long for him to come back and then I would take matters into my own hands. But I don't know what I would do."

Caleb said, "Too much coincidence here. Brady must know something about the killings."

"And," Samantha said, "he insisted we should not go to the law. He would not say why, and he thought it was dangerous for us to know more. He said Mister Gaines would know what to do. He has always set a lot of store in the banker."

Sarah sighed, "I know he has. I don't know why."

Samantha said, "They are friends. Maybe Mister Gaines is like a father to him. Anyway, they have grown-up talks about business things, and somebody named Adam Smith."

"I know," Sarah said. "Matt Gaines gave Brady a Smith book. *Wealth of Nations*, I think it is called. Most of it sounds quite boring to me."

"I think someone should go to Mister Gaines," Samantha said.

"That would be me," Sarah said, dreading the prospect of talking to the banker about Brady's dilemma. But Matthew Gains knew people and seemingly had accumulated considerable wealth. She knew precisely how to get his attention. Maybe it was time.

Caleb pointed out. "You would be followed. That could complicate things. Sammy and I will ride into town tomorrow. I will go to Oaks General Store and pick up extra supplies. I can tell Jeb I forgot some things when I was in today in case somebody asks about me. Sammy can go to the bank. Nobody would think anything about her going there to run an errand. She can ask to talk to Gaines and give him a note from you that explains the problem and that you want to speak with him. I am betting he can figure out a way to do things without raising curiosity from the wrong folks."

"I will have something in the morning."

Samantha said, "I will come over and take care of the cats and do the other chores right after sunrise. I've helped Brady plenty of times and know what to do."

Caleb asked, "Do you want to stay with us tonight, Sarah?"

"No, if I am being watched, that would raise more suspicion and endanger your family even more. I have a question, though."

"Yes?"

"James Tolliver was very polite and a total gentleman, but he asked a lot of questions about Brady. I even told him Brady would head into the mountains. Do you think Tolliver is with the killers that are looking for him?"

"I'm sorry to say, it seems likely. I'm just glad he didn't harm you. I wouldn't be offering any more meals to strangers."

"Would you mind loading Brady's double-barreled shotgun before you go?"

# Chapter 5

JOHN TRACE CROCKETT, dressed smartly in a new blue suit, black boots and string bow tie, sat at his desk near the window in the Crockett Detective Agency offices in downtown Manhattan, Kansas. The agency facilities consisted of two rooms and a closet, a large front office with desks to accommodate four detectives and a smaller conference room to the rear for private meetings. The offices were rented from Suzanne Carter, a young woman who operated a barbershop in the other half of the limestone building.

It was what local farmers and ranchers called an Indian summer day in early October of 1882, and the Flint Hills beckoned. He had planned to work with his two hired hands to cut and stack hay from a portion of the nearly one thousand acres of tall grass prairie that had not been pastured on the two sections of land owned by

Three Winds Ranch. Three Winds was a land partnership formed by Trace, his wife, Darby Maguire Crockett, and Audra Scott, the detective agency partners. Mostly grass, the 1,280 acres included a nice spring-fed creek and pond, along which grew lowland oaks and cottonwoods that furnished nice winter shelter for the cattle herd.

He did not even hear Darby come in the door, and she startled him when she spoke with just a hint of an Irish lilt. "Since they put up the hardware store next door, you've got about ten feet of dry weeds and a limestone wall to study outside that window."

He wheeled the swivel chair around and smiled sheepishly at the woman with wheat-blonde, shoulder length hair and dark brown eyes looking impishly at him through wire-rimmed spectacles. When she left for work this morning astride Cinnamon, her blood bay gelding, she had been attired in faded denims, a plaid wool shirt, scuffed boots, and a tattered low-crowned hat tugged down on her forehead. Since then, she had changed into a charcoal-gray skirt with matching jacket and a white blouse and appeared very businesslike. She was a stunning woman however she dressed.

One wall of the conference room was curtained off to conceal a closet that ran the length of the room where Trace and Darby stored their business wardrobes, or "town clothes," as Trace called them. Trace's suits and boots, frequently replaced, claimed two-thirds of the rack and floor space. Darby, a penny pincher, dressed tastefully but required noticeable wear to abandon a garment and was satisfied with a few pairs of alternating shoes.

"I was thinking deep thoughts," Trace said.

Darby sat down at her own desk, which was no more than five feet from his. "I'm not even going to ask you about your thoughts. We can't act upon them at the moment anyway."

"There's the conference room table," Trace teased.

"We tried that, remember? And the table leg broke, and you fell off and hurt your back. You were out of service for a week, and I had to come up with a white lie to explain the table damage to Audra. And she just laughed and said tables were intended for 'sitting at,' not 'lying on.'"

"Blaming it on termites was not a very creative lie," he said. "But contrary to your assumption, I was pondering things I should be doing at the ranch. We've got a hundred new bred Red Angus cows and heifers to feed this winter that the C Bar C will be driving to our place next week. We'll have a herd to get through the winter. I didn't want to stock the ranch till spring, but that woman who runs the place said she wouldn't be doing business with anybody for those cows if she had to feed them all winter. She has a big operation, but she was way overstocked. She also needed money, as most ranchers do, and she made me a fair deal."

"And now we're the ones who need money. We've got Jimmy Dale starting the new house and bunkhouse any day. We could use a good assignment right now." Jimmy Dale was their barber landlord's fiancée and a young craftsman and builder, who had agreed to construct a house on their ranch to replace the two-room dugout that had come with the land. The roof leaked like a sieve, and Trace planned to put his cowhands to work on repairs that would see the Crocketts through the winter.

"The T Bar down the road will let Herb and Buck bunk there as long as necessary—not as convenient as we'd like, but it takes the pressure off some," Trace said.

"I've lived in Kansas some winters now, and that dugout won't work in its sorry shape. We've got to find a place in town to winter."

"Herb and Buck will get it patched up. Herb's done some carpentry. We're paying them anyhow. Think of the housing costs we can save if we don't have to stay in town." Trace knew that money was her Achilles heel and felt he was getting more adept at using that little tool during their occasional differences.

"We'll see," Darby replied, noncommittally.

He quickly changed the subject. "So, what do you think Carl has got for us?"

"The telegram just said his train would arrive at the Manhattan station shortly after one o'clock, and he would be at our office by two. And we should be ready to depart tomorrow morning. That's it."

"No time to make arrangements here."

"We're in the detective business, remember? Our jobs can't be planned weeks in advance," she said. "And we need a new assignment to support your cows and build a house."

Trace sighed and plucked his timepiece from his pocket. "It's past one-thirty. He should be here soon."

Darby said, "I'm betting he will be here before two o'clock. The ATSF has been right on schedule the past few months."

No sooner had she spoken than the office door opened and a stocky man carrying a battered, leather briefcase and wearing a rumpled business suit and derby hat limped in. "I didn't take your bet," Trace said, as he stood and waved the visitor in.

He stepped toward his former boss and extended his hand. "Carl, good to see you." They exchanged firm grips before Darby pushed Trace aside and gave the man a warm hug and a soft kiss on the cheek.

The man with translucent blue eyes and a cherubic face almost surrendered a rare smile. He removed his hat, brushing back the few mussed tufts of white hair that remained on a shiny scalp. "Conference room?" he asked, nodding toward the door of the room he had shared with them on previous occasions. Without waiting for an answer, he headed toward their meeting place.

Carl Chirnside was the manager of the Kansas City field office of Pinkerton's National Detective Agency. He directed most Pinkerton operations between Kansas City and Denver and north and south of the line between the two cities. He had been confined to case assignment and management for some years due to effects of a gunshot wound to his knee when he and other Pinkerton agents thwarted an assassination attempt on President Lincoln during the Civil War years. But Trace respected the man and liked him despite Chirnside's brusque demeanor.

Chirnside claimed the chair at the head of the table and dropped his bulging briefcase in front of him, and Trace and Darby took chairs on each side of him. Darby had picked up her pencil and notebook at her desk and had those at the ready. Trace rarely wrote anything down. His wife more than made up for his disdain for the written record, he figured, since she produced enough pages during an investigation to fill several books.

Chirnside placed his hat on the table next to the briefcase, opened the leather bag and withdrew a single sheet of paper. He handed it to Darby. "I know Darby can read," he said, needling Trace a bit. "This is all I have for you beyond my spoken words. That sheet outlines the best routes to your destination and what little I know about your contact there."

"You are assuming we will take your assignment," Trace said. "Our agency is independent, remember?"

"And what percentage of your revenue comes from anyone other than Pinkerton?" Chirnside retorted.

Darby intervened. "This says our assignment takes us to Lockwood, Wyoming. Mountain valley town, it appears. The contact is one Matthew Gaines. Banker. Forty-five years old. Owns all the stock of the Gaines Bank. Has some landholdings in the valley and investment properties in town. Financially comfortable, it seems, but doesn't quite cross the bridge to wealthy by most standards. Maybe on the road to riches. What do you know about the killings and the missing boy?"

"Nothing more than what's on the paper. Sheriff and a woman were murdered. Boy is missing. Gaines wants an outside investigation, and, if the boy hasn't been found by the time you get there, he wants you to head up a search. Telegram said urgent. We replied with a fee estimate and he wired approval. Sounded like a perfect job for the blood hounds."

Money. That was Darby's end of the business. Trace decided to let her continue the discussion on their part. It was an unnecessary decision. She moved in instantly for the kill.

"You pay expenses, train travel, lodging, meals and other out-of-pocket expenses for a start," Darby said.

"I expected that," Chirnside replied.

"Two hundred dollars a day. That will cover Trace and me. As you know, Audra and Clay are on a Pinkerton job in Arkansas."

"I was thinking half that."

"No dickering. We're thinking of going totally independent, giving Pinkerton some competition."

Trace did not recall any discussion about that.

Chirnside frowned and was silent for a moment. "You are getting a little greedy, don't you think, Darby?"

Trace was glad her dark eyes were not snapping at him like they were at Chirnside right now.

"Greedy? I would like to talk to Allan Pinkerton about greed. We make him huge profits on every job."

"But you wouldn't have the big jobs without the Pinkerton connection. And the company has a huge payroll around the country. You do want Pinkerton to stay in business, don't you?"

"So we are agreed on the two hundred?"

Chirnside sighed heavily. "Yeah. Two hundred per diem."

Darby said, "Now, let's finish this up with the bonuses."

Chirnside gave her a look of disbelief. "Bonuses? After you bled us like a vampire on the per diem?"

"You've been fair on that. Tell me that Pinkerton Agency doesn't have a bonus coming for results."

"We will pay twenty-five hundred if you locate the boy. Nothing if he shows up before you get there. Another twenty-five hundred if you find the killers of the sheriff and the woman," Chirnside said.

"Three thousand each, and we've got a deal."

"Three thousand? But you aren't leaving any profit for the Pinkerton Agency. You do remember the job out in No Man's Land? You got a bonus when that Sanford gal did more to find you than you did to find her."

"We brought her back," Darby countered. "I'm sure Pinkerton claimed a much larger bonus before Allan paid out our share. He should get it all for sitting on his butt in the Chicago office?"

"And now she's going to work for you. You came out on that deal okay."

"What do you mean?" Trace asked. "Maddie Sanford doesn't work for us."

"That's what she told me," Chirnside said. "I got acquainted with her on the ATSF during my trip here this morning. Had a big, big dog with her. She said the animal was at least half wolf, and I believe it. She talked up a storm. I didn't believe half of what she said, but she's a likable gal. Pretty little thing."

Trace said, "Well, she's not working for us. Last I knew, she was living with her father in Kansas City and going to a private girl's school there."

"Well, she got off the train when I did, and I haven't seen a sign of her since I left the station."

# Chapter 6

ARBY HEARD THE front door of the Crockett Detective Agency office open as she finished filling in the blanks and deleting and adding provisions to the pre-printed contracts furnished by the Pinkerton Agency. She and Trace signed on behalf of their firm and Carl Chirnside entered his signature for Pinkerton.

"I'll check the door," Trace said. He got up and left the conference room.

Darby and Chirnside shook hands and exchanged parting pleasantries before following Trace to the front office, where they found Trace chatting amicably with a young woman with short-cropped, chestnut hair, green eyes and a coltish figure. She was accompanied by a huge, short-haired dog with erect ears. Pirate, named for the black hair about one eye that gave the appearance of an eye patch. The creature had fur of a calico coloring with splotches of bluish-black, orange and white splotches merging over his body. But the eerie yellow eyes were what would first grab any observer's attention.

Maddie Sanford's face flushed when she saw Carl Chirnside. "Mister Chirnside," she said. "I didn't know you had business here."

"Nice to see you again, young lady," Chirnside said. "I hope things work out well for you with the Crockett Agency. I wish I could chat some more, but I must be on my way." He made a quick exit out the doorway.

"Hello, Maddie," Darby said, moving to the girl and giving her a quick hug. "This is a surprise. We're glad to see you, but I thought you were in school."

"I was. I quit. I hated it there. Hitchcock is a private girls' school. It's a boarding school, so I had to live at the campus. My three roommates were prigs and made fun of my love for ranching and the outdoors. They called me 'hayseed.'"

Darby thought none of her friends at the school could have survived the ordeal the fifteen-year-old Maddie had undergone when abducted during a train robbery several months back. This young lady was as gritty as any person, young or old, she had ever known. "What does your father say about this?"

"He doesn't know yet unless the school notified him at the ATSF offices. I sneaked out of my room before sunrise and headed for Daddy's house five miles from the school. They kept Pirate in a doghouse there inside a board fence no more than five by ten feet. It broke my heart to see him like that when I went home weekends. No way for a wild creature like him to be cared for."

"I'm sure your father meant well, but a big dog like that can't just be turned loose to roam in town," Darby said.

"I suppose, but I know he hated it. And he looked so sad. And I am a ranch girl, I don't belong in the city locked up in a female prison. Anyhow, I hid in the storage shed till Daddy left for work. I knew the housekeeper wouldn't come till at least an hour later, and I slipped in, ditched my school uniform and dressed up like a respectable lady. Then I packed what my carpet bag would hold and got all the money I had stashed from my secret wall hidey-hole. After that, I got Pirate from his jail and we walked until I caught a four-wheel cab to take us to the station. I purchased two tickets to Manhattan, and here I am."

Maddie's parents were divorced and had resided on a small ranch outside of Denver until their parting a few years earlier. During the ranch years, Thomas Sanford, her father, who was a vice-president and major shareholder of the Atchison, Topeka and Santa Fe Railroad Company, worked out of the Denver office. He had transferred to the Kansas City office after the divorce, and Maddie had remained with her mother, who resided in a Denver hotel-residence complex. Mother and daughter were at war from the beginning, and the mother finally surrendered. Alexandra Sanford had put her daughter on board a train and sent her to live with her father the day it was robbed, and Maddie was taken by the notorious Blue Bandana Gang.

"Your father will be worried sick about you," Darby said.

"I left a note on the desk in his study. That's the first place he goes when he gets home."

"What on earth did you tell him?"

"That I was going back to Mother's."

Darby said, "But that was a lie. A few telegrams will make that clear. And he is with the railroad. He should be able to find out where you went."

"I suppose. But by that time, I will be self-supporting."

"But you are only fifteen," Darby said. "You aren't . . . emancipated. You have to do what your folks say."

"My folks can't even agree on what to do with me. And I read up on this in the school library. They have the Kansas and Missouri statutes there. In Kansas I am emancipated at age eighteen or when I become self-supporting, whichever happens first. If I am not a vagrant on the streets, nobody is going to arrest me and take me back to my father. There are thousands of kids my age living on their own."

"Are you sure you weren't attending law school?"

"Of course not, but I think I might like being a lawyer if I could have my ranch, too," Maddie replied.

She would probably make a hell of a good one, too, Darby thought.

Trace, who had remained silent during the conversation between the two, said, "The man who just left the office was Carl Chirnside. He is the manager of the Pinkerton National Detective Agency Kansas City office. We are contract Pinkerton agents, and most of our work comes by way of assignments from Carl. He said that you told him you had a job here."

Maddie shrugged and rolled her eyes. "I guess I exaggerated some. I was coming here to apply for a job."

"Maddie," Darby said, "we are leaving for Wyoming tomorrow on an assignment. The other agents are on assignment elsewhere. I'm sure we can arrange for you to stay at the Wheaton mansion with Elisabeth Denney till we return. After your last stay, she said you would always be welcome there."

"Why don't Pirate and I go with you? We won't be in your way, and we'll prove our worth. I wouldn't expect any pay."

Darby thought a moment. She looked at Trace, whose stoic expression betrayed nothing. He had dropped this problem in her lap. "Trace, we need to talk," she said, nodding toward the conference room. "Maddie, take one of the chairs and wait."

"Yes, ma'am."

When they stepped into the conference room and closed the door, Darby said, "Well?"

"Well, what?"

"You've been quiet. Do you have an opinion about this?"

"That gal's tough as rawhide. Smart as a whip. And Pirate might come in handy. He'll look after Maddie anyway."

"You are okay with her coming with us?"

"Yeah, I'm okay with it."

"I admit I'm fond of the girl, and I can't see her being a burden. And I don't know what else to do with her right now. Let's take the pair along. We aren't going to pay her anything, though. We can handle expenses. That's it." She opened the door, and Trace followed her back to the front office area.

Maddie stood when they returned, her demeanor more subdued now. She looked at Trace and he winked. She returned a nervous smile.

"I saw that," Darby said. "Yes, Maddie. You can go with us. No pay, but the Crockett firm will cover all expenses. You can come home with us now, but the accommodations are barely habitable. You will have to sleep on the parlor floor tonight. We will put together a bedroll for you."

Maddie grinned. "You can't give me worse accommodations than I had in No Man's Land."

"I suppose not." She turned to Trace. "What about the horses? Do they travel with us?"

"I don't think so," he said. "Carl said there is still a stage line running from Laramie to Lockwood with stop-offs at relay stations along the way. I don't know how much time we'll be horseback, and it will save a lot of hassle if we don't have to worry about horse care and transfers along the way. I'm sure there will be a livery where we can rent mounts if we need them, horses that are used to mountain country."

Darby said, "I'll see if I can get tickets for the first train headed to Denver tomorrow. And I will check with Suzanne to be sure it is all right for us to post a sign on the door to check with her if somebody is looking for us.

I'll tell her we will telegraph contact information as soon as we arrive in Lockwood if she needs to get hold of us."

"I need to head back to the ranch," Trace said, "and talk to Herb and Buck about what they can be working on while I'm gone. Fortunately, Buck's been around the cattle business a long time and would probably do fine without my instructions . . . maybe better. They'll have their hands full when that cowgirl and her hands drive the Red Angus herd to the Three Winds."

"You go on ahead. I'll rent a horse for Maddie, and after we've taken care of the things in town, we'll join you at the house."

Trace slipped into the conference room to change into his riding clothes. Darby turned to Maddie and made a quick appraisal of the girl. At about five feet, six inches tall, Maddie was near her own height but on the skinny side and not so full in the hips and butt. That would take care of itself soon enough, Darby figured. Anyhow, she should be able to scavenge some clothes for the girl from her own things.

"Okay, Maddie, you and your friend can come with me. We're going to the telegraph office first, and you are going to wire your father and tell him where you're at and assure him you have a temporary job and will be writing a letter tonight to post in the morning."

"A letter?"

"Yes. You can do that tonight. Tell him you are working on a Pinkerton job with the Crockett Detective Agency and whatever else you want to say. Assure him that you
love him, but you should let him know how you really feel
about your life and what you want to do. I will give you
our address, so he can write to you here, and, perhaps
you will have a letter waiting when you get back. Then
you can sort things out between you. Maybe a bit of separation will do you both good."

"I really have to write a letter?"

"You do. That is your first Pinkerton assignment. After we take care of the telegram, we will get the train tickets and then come back here. I will give you a Pinkerton
badge and fill in some pre-signed credentials and see if
we can find you some riding clothes and a business outfit
or two in the closet. The flowered dress you are wearing is
a pretty thing, but we want to find something more pro-
fessional looking, an outfit that will age you up a little. I
do carry a make-up kit in my disguise bag, so I can work
on your face some before we get to Lockwood."

"You do disguises? That sounds like fun."

"Trace doesn't think so, but I saved his hide with one
in Dodge City before we were married. I worked in the

theatre some in Boston before I came west, and I worked with makeup when I wasn't acting."

"You were an actress?"

"Never made a nickel at it, but it was fun. I ended up a schoolteacher. A long story."

"I'd love to hear it."

"Maybe someday, when the time is right."

It occurred to Darby that maybe the estrangement from her own parents had something to do with her willingness to take this girl under her wing.

# Chapter 7

TRACE WAITED IN the parlor of "Sally's Bed & Board," a homey two-story, clapboard rooming house at the south end of Main Street in Lockwood, Wyoming. His mind wandered wistfully, however, to the luxurious appearing "Mountain Inn" across the street. He and Darby never disagreed to the point of serious verbal battle, but they occasionally fussed a bit when it came to money. Trace had a penchant for first class when it came to lodging, clothing, dining or other lifestyle preferences. He could not help but chide his beautiful, otherwise considerate and patient, wife, for being a skinflint at such times. However, she indulged his wardrobe extravagance without serious complaint, so his grumbling on matters like this were essentially token.

He had pointed out, however, that the Pinkertons would be absorbing the cost, and the Crocketts would not incur expense as the result of raising standards some. He had shut his mouth upon receiving her stern look. Frugality was engrained in Darby Maguire Crockett, and it mattered not whose money was involved.

He had to admit, though, that Sally's was a clean and comfortable place, and he was being quickly seduced by the redolent aroma of something almost constantly baking. The cost of three meals a day was included in the rent, so Trace was certain Darby would be reluctant to explore other eating opportunities in the town. He vowed to think of a special occasion she could not resist.

The stage ride from Laramie to Lockwood had taken most of a long day and was without question the most grueling part of the nearly three-day journey. The speed and relative comfort of trains by comparison could spoil a man. He supposed trains would become faster and yet more comfortable, and as rail connections increased, stagecoach travel would become increasingly rare, but there would always be a place for horses, wagons and other such short distance transportation. And a train could not be used to plant and harvest crops or herd cattle.

They had arrived late afternoon the previous day and found the boardinghouse just in time for supper. Sally was a buxom middle-aged woman with black, gray-streaked hair, lightly bronzed skin and aquiline nose and features that suggested Indian lineage. She had studied the newcomers with dark, inquisitive eyes before renting two rooms but had asked no questions about their purpose in Lockwood. She had assessed an additional fifty cents daily for Pirate's shared occupancy of Maddie's room.

Trace had no complaints about the food, and he was still stuffed from the hearty breakfast of pancakes, sausages, eggs and perfect, fresh coffee they had enjoyed an hour earlier. They were due at the Gaines Bank at nine o'clock, a half hour from now, and Darby was "preparing" Maddie for their meeting with the banker, whatever that meant. Fortunately, Sally had taken a liking to Pirate and had agreed that the wolfdog could remain with her while her other boarders were out on business. Trace had worried that the big, unusual-appearing dog might attract too much attention to their visit.

Shortly, Darby and an older version of Maddie appeared, both attired in skirts and jackets appropriate to business wear. Trace could not determine how the transformation had taken place in Maddie. Her face had been somehow slimmed down, and the freckles that dusted her nose had disappeared. Her eyebrows were darker and more refined. Perhaps, the small felt hat that was perched atop her head and pinned to her hair was part of it. Whatever had happened, the girl had been aged ten years to where she appeared only a few years younger than Darby's recently attained twenty-seven.

"What do you think?" Darby asked, as Trace stood to greet his companions.

"I think I have the pleasure of escorting two beautiful women to the bank. But what did you do with the girl who came with us?"

"She is hiding for the moment."

Maddie beamed, obviously enjoying her new role.

"I hope Matthew Gaines received the message we sent with the boy last night," Trace said.

"I'm sure he did," Darby said. "The man at the general store where we disembarked said the boy makes his living that way, waiting around the store for an opportunity to run errands, help load supplies or carry messages for folks. He was probably at least twelve. I am sure Gaines received the sealed envelope at his home. I wrote where we would be staying in the event he wanted to schedule a different place or time."

"But we hadn't decided where we were going to stay yet when you sent the message . . . oh, I see. I had already lost the debate before we had our little discussion, hadn't I?"

"Trace, I just trusted in your unfailing good judgment to see things my way."

# Chapter 8

MATTHEW GAINES HAD received the message regarding the Pinkerton agents' arrival, and they were now seated in his office at a small round table set off from his desk. It was a discreet way, Trace thought, of putting all participants on an equal footing, establishing an intimacy that was absent when one party sat like a king behind a big desk.

Gaines was a soft-spoken man with salt and pepper hair and blue eyes that expressed a gentleness that matched his voice. He stood an inch or two under six feet, and his gray suit covered a frame that seemed trim and fit.

Trace took the lead, "Mister Gaines . . ."

"Please, make it Matt."

"Matt. And we will be Trace, Darby and Maddie. I'm certain you are aware that we don't have much information about the nature of our mission here. Your telegram was extremely vague, but I am guessing necessarily so. And it's difficult to transmit much detail that way, anyhow. Beats the days of Pony Express, though. Regardless, the Pinkerton home office was interested enough to send us here."

Gaines smiled. "Money does talk, doesn't it?"

"I wouldn't deny it. Your message made mention of a missing boy. Has he shown up?"

"No. the boy's name is Brady Yates. Most around here call him 'Trouble.'"

"I don't understand. Why is he trouble?"

"It's a nickname picked up from school days. He is a fine boy, unbelievably hard working and enterprising for a thirteen-year-old. Extremely bright. And I must insist you keep in confidence what I am going to say next."

"As long as it involves nothing illegal, you can rely on confidentiality regarding anything you say in the room," Trace assured him.

"Brady Yates is my son," Gaines said, his voice so soft Trace could barely hear him.

Trace waited, sensing Gaines had a story to tell.

Gaines continued. "I did not know Brady was my son until several days ago, shortly before I sent the telegram to the Pinkerton office. I had befriended the youngster almost three years ago when he opened an account here. I saw something of my youthful self in him in his almost driving need to work and seek out opportunities to make a dollar. Some of us just don't do well in a rocking chair, and Brady and I are kindred spirits that way. I loved teaching him about money and how it worked in our system. He was even fascinated with economic theories, and I shared some of Adam Smith's works with him. Imagine that. A mere boy interested in that stuff. I don't know of anyone else in town who has likely read Adam Smith, with perhaps the exception of my lawyer friend, Ethan Ramsey."

"Adam Smith is an old friend of mine from economics class at West Point," Trace said, "but would not be my choice for leisurely reading."

"Oh, I am impressed. A West Point graduate."

"No, I am afraid not, and my Army service was in the Comanche wars as a non-commissioned officer." Trace was not about to tell the man about his senior year expulsion for a dalliance with a professor's wife. "Please, continue. Tell us whatever you are comfortable discussing."

Gaines said, "I just wanted you to know the young man was special to me before I learned I was his father. My wife and I have no children, and I thought of Brady as the son I never had. You can imagine how overwhelmed

I was when I learned he, in fact, is my son, my flesh and blood son."

"And that is why you were willing to spend so much money to find him," Trace said.

"Yes and no. For Brady, I would have done this anyway. But it is far more complicated than that. You must wonder how I suddenly became aware of my paternity. Well, the morning following Brady's disappearance, I received a note from Brady's mother, Sarah Yates, that it was urgent that I speak with her and that I come to her home disguised as a cowhand as Sarah said she was being watched, and I would not wish to be identified. It was all very mysterious, and I did not know that Brady was missing."

Trace said, "She knew how to grab your attention."

"I was in love with Sarah once. I felt I owed her. She didn't need to induce me to answer a summons. I am happily married. Martha knows about my earlier relationship with Sarah. I told her about the message, and she understood I had to respond. The two serious romances in my life have been with women who are far better persons than I."

"So you went to Sarah's home?"

"Yes, of course. The disguise was no problem. I have a small cattle operation, and I am a working rancher when

I am not in the bank. I was armed when I rode out to the Yates farm. I was a Union officer during the War of the Rebellion, and I can handle weapons if need be. But I hope my killing days are over." He paused for a moment before continuing. "I went to her home and seeing her was bittersweet. She is still beautiful, a decade younger than I am, I suppose. But that day she was using a cane, and I noticed tremors in her hands and fingers as she spoke. She was thinner, but she was not wasted away as some folks have claimed."

Darby spoke for the first time. "She is ill?"

"Not specifically diagnosed. Brady told me the doctor says there is nothing to be done for it. It is a condition folks occasionally come down with, but there is not even a name for the disease or whatever it is. I guess she has good days, and it is worse when she is under stress, which she is certainly dealing with now."

Darby said, "My aunt had such a condition."

Gaines continued. "Anyway, Sarah told me immediately why she had sent for me. She informed me in a very matter of fact way that Brady is my son. I was a single man when we first met, and she was operating a tailoring business in town. She fitted me for a suit, and I was overwhelmed by her beauty and charm. And keen intelligence. She was married, had been for several years. But her husband was frequently gone for extended periods. I purchased more suits than I could afford during this time and made it my business to know when Alfred Yates was absent. One day I just happened to be riding by her place on a Sunday afternoon and dropped by to chat. The rest is history as they say. I saw her for a year or more whenever Alfred was gone. I begged her to divorce him and marry me. I know he beat her and that she furnished virtually all their financial support. We loved each other. I guess it was a tawdry thing by most standards, but I take the blame. I was the pursuer. She was a lonely, vulnerable woman."

"But something happened to change things?" Trace asked.

"Yes. Alfred came home and stayed for several months. I intercepted her on the trail to their farm after work one day and asked her again to leave him and marry me. Alfred had been back just a few days. She told me it was over. She had spoken with a lawyer and was told she must have grounds and that she had none. She said it was a sin to do what we had been doing, and she would not live that way. I was not to call on her again, and I was not welcome in her shop. I was broken hearted but took her at her word."

"And you didn't see her again?" Darby said.

"Not romantically or illicitly. I would encounter her on the street, and we would exchange perfunctory greetings, but it was over." He twisted his lips wryly. "But I guess it is not."

"You don't really know that the boy is yours," Trace said.

"I believe her, and it all makes sense. Brady's birthdate would fit with the last several times Sarah and I were . . . uh . . . together. True, it would have fit the time when her husband first returned home, but she said they didn't have relations. He was ill when he came home. Had a fever, sore throat, aching muscles and was exhausted. But what frightened her was a pox about his neck and face. Without asking, when she was in town, she asked the doctor to come out. It turns out that the pox and blisters covered his . . . pardon me ladies . . . male organs."

"Syphilis," Trace said. "I saw a lot of that in the Army."

"Yes, and she did not allow him near her that visit and declared she never would. She slept in the parlor the month or so he was there, always with a gun by her side. He disappeared after that and didn't return for a year. When he found her with the baby, he beat her half to death because he knew the child could not be his. She couldn't go to the law without causing a scandal. When he was drinking at the table after he had beaten her nearly senseless, she got to her Winchester, placed the barrel against his head and told him to leave. If he stayed, she said he had better not sleep, because he would never wake up. She was very matter of fact when she told me this."

Trace said, "So he left?"

"Yes. She says she never saw him again. After five or six years, Ethan Ramsey, her lawyer, helped her go to court and have Alfred declared dead, and she got title to the farm cleared in her name. About this same time, she began to have symptoms of this disease that plagues her. Eventually, she was forced to give up her tailoring business, but she knew how to manage money and eked out a living from her savings and farm rents. Not long after, Brady began taking on odd jobs and taking on projects to earn money, and they never really suffered that much financially." He smiled. "For the past several years, he's been raising cats, selling kittens for ratters and making good money at it."

"And Alfred just disappeared?" Darby asked.

"Well, most of us never saw him again, and Sarah says she did not."

Darby said, "You sound doubtful."

"Well, at least two people I know of claim to have seen him three or four years ago. The county recorder is one of them. He says that Alfred was in the office checking on title to the property and was upset to find it was in Sarah's name. He was wanting to force Sarah to buy him out or put the place up for sale, so he could get some cash out of it according to the recorder. He left in a rage, but nobody ever saw him after that."

Trace said, "Well, I guess that's none of our concern. Tell us why we're looking for this boy."

"I will. But I want you to understand something. If I had known that Sarah was carrying my child, I would have found a way to marry her and raise my son. I didn't meet Martha until a few years later. Sarah was in my heart until I found love again. Even after that, I would have supported my son if she had just told me. She maintains that she just did not want public shame or embarrassment for either of us—or for Brady to be the object of scandal. Sarah insisted she was capable of making it on her own, which, of course, she was. She is a remarkable woman. I hope that by calling you folks in, I can help make things up to her in a small way. And selfishly, I want to find Brady."

Darby asked, "So how did this come about? He wasn't abducted?"

"No. He saw something. Evidently knows something that put his life in danger. You must talk to a neighbor girl his age, Samantha Morris. Her parents, Caleb and Millie Morris, and their family live across the river from Sarah and Brady. She is the last person to speak with Brady before he disappeared. And a man came by looking for Brady not long after his stop there. I'm not sure if she has told all she knows or not, but she knows Brady better than anybody. She did say, however, that the reason Brady left was that he saw something and that he was going to hide in the mountains until he figured out what to do. And Brady told her that they should not go to the law about his being gone."

"Strange. Sounds ominous," Darby said, as her pencil point raced across the pages of her notebook.

"It's not difficult to draw a conclusion with a few more facts," Gaines said. "The same day Brady disappeared, our county sheriff and a woman were murdered at her house off the road that eventually leads to the Yates place. Also, I forgot to mention that someone is watching Sarah's house. That worries me sick. You don't have to be a detective to conclude that Brady saw something and that the killers know it. Now why he didn't want Samantha to go to the law—that has me scratching my head a bit."

"Sheriff's name?" Darby asked.

"Will Bridges. Older fellow. Sheriff all the fifteen years I've been in Lockwood. Good man. Highly respected."

"Woman?"

"Lucy Brisbane. A nice woman by all accounts. Late twenties or early thirties. I don't like saying this in mixed company, but she was a painted woman."

"A prostitute?" Darby asked.

"Well, it wasn't like she had a sign on her door. She took visitors at her home and carried on her life like a respectable lady, you might say. See her in the bank or the general store, you would never guess. But folks knew. Some, but not all, of the ladies looked down on her and would not speak to her. But most men didn't treat her any different." He shrugged and surrendered a small smile. "If they weren't with their wives."

"Do you think the sheriff was a customer, client or whatever you would call her visitors?" Darby asked.

"I would be surprised. Will was widowed not many years back. Several widow ladies were on his trail, but he seemed to have no interest. But who can really say? Who knows what is in someone's mind or heart and how a person might find comfort or solace? I'm slow to judge folks, and I would not think less of Will if he did visit Lucy on occasion, but I am still reluctant to believe he was there as a customer. Doesn't fit the man I knew."

"And who represents the law in Lockwood now?" Trace asked.

Gaines replied, "One deputy sheriff. His name is Ferd Bullock. The town doesn't have a separate marshal. The county provides the law enforcement. I happen to be the town's mayor, and I sent a telegram to the U. S. Marshal's office in Cheyenne requesting an investigation of the sheriff's killing but, so far, no response. I was going to follow up after I spoke with you folks."

Darby said, "Tell us about Bullock."

Gaines shrugged. "Early fifties. He has been deputy a dozen years, I suppose. Probably okay as a deputy in a peaceful town. Not qualified to be top dog. Some people are best suited for following instructions. Ferd would be one of those. At first, he might come off as dimwitted. But he's smarter than he acts or looks. I think Will knew that and was able to use Ferd where his abilities fit."

"But if Brady warned against going to the law," Trace said, "he must have been talking about Bullock."

"It would seem so. That's why I have avoided the man awaiting your arrival. I will leave it to you to approach him or give your thoughts on what I should do. I am at your disposal."

Darby said, "So you really want us not only to find Brady but to identify the sheriff's killer or killers?"

"That, yes, and why. I can't put my finger on it, but I'm convinced the story behind Will's death is important to the entire community."

"I agree," Trace said. "If this was just a revenge killing by some hired guns, why do the killers even care about Brady Yates? They would just move on and disappear. With a boy as the only witness, there's not much chance they would ever be identified and arrested."

# Chapter 9

THE DETECTIVES SPENT the better part of the morning discussing the missing boy and the sheriff's murder with Matthew Gaines. After departing the bank, they returned to Sally's Bed & Board for noon dinner and joined five other guests for a feast of fresh-baked bread, roast beef and gravy, boiled potatoes, pinto beans, and apple cobbler. During their absence, Sally and Pirate had formed a fast bond, and the big wolf-dog enjoyed a huge bowl of meat scraps in the separate kitchen. With the presence of the other guests in the dining room, their conversation had necessarily remained casual, but when the meal was finished, they adjourned to the Crockett room to talk.

Trace sat on the edge of the bed and surrendered the two straight-back chairs to the ladies. Pirate leaped upon the bed and stretched out behind him for a post-dinner snooze. "Here's what I'm thinking," Trace said. "Speak up if you disagree."

"Do you really think I would not?" Darby said.

Trace did not respond. "I think we should be in the saddle by sunrise tomorrow morning to start the search for Trouble Yates. But we have some groundwork first. Darby, you are the best interrogator. I suggest you interview Deputy Bullock at his office. Matt was confident the man is holing up there right now. After that, perhaps, you can talk to someone at the Ramsey and Locke law firm. There will be some confidentiality limitations on what anyone there can say, I suppose, but Matt said they can be trusted and might be helpful. I wonder if the Locke partner is related to our Manhattan lawyers. Not likely, I guess."

"I can do that."

"We'll be presenting our credentials, so before the day is out half the town will know we are Pinkertons. You will want a pistol in your bag."

She rolled her eyes and gave him an annoyed look. "My Baby Russian has been in my bag all morning, and my Derringer is strapped to my thigh." She would bet if Maddie had not been in the room, he would have asked her to prove up on the Derringer.

"Maddie and I are going to get in riding clothes and take the trail along the North Laramie River. Along the way, I want to take a gander at the house where the sheriff and lady were killed. Then we're going to ride on to the Yates and Morris farms and split off. I think Maddie would be best to talk to Samantha Morris, being closer to the girl's age and all. I'm going to have a little visit with the man watching the Yates house and then we will rendezvous at Missus Yates's house."

"Trace," Darby said, "you're not going to kill anybody, are you?"

"Hope not. I'm going to use my powers of persuasion. I expect the man to decide it is the better part of wisdom for him to give up his spying job."

"I don't like it."

"How do you think that woman must feel staying there by her lonesome with some varmint up in the hills watching every move? Do you want me to just let it go?"

"No. But I think killing somebody would make things worse fast."

"I agree. Now let's get about our business. Matt recommended Fletcher's Livery for the best horses. Maddie, go get changed into your riding garb. Grab your rifle and scabbard and we'll go see what this Enos Fletcher has for horseflesh."

After Maddie left with Pirate, Darby stood by silently while Trace changed into his denim britches, checkered cotton shirt, and scuffed boots. Quite a transformation, she thought, from suited dandy of a few minutes earlier. But he was still a mouth-watering specimen. "Better take your buckskin jacket with you," she said, "the mountain air will chill fast late afternoon, especially along the river bottom."

"Yes, Mother."

He bristled at her reminders, but sometimes he was a child about such things. Ten minutes out, he would have been complaining about the cold if he didn't take a coat. She walked over to where he stood next to the bed, wrapped her arms around his neck, pulled his head toward hers and gave him a warm kiss on welcoming lips.

Trace stepped back and looked at her with feigned annoyance. "You are always a tease when we don't have time. You've got a streak of cruelty in you."

"Don't get shot, and I will make it up to you tonight."

"Powerful incentive."

# Chapter 10

TROUBLE YATES HAD been holed up for over a week in the cave he and Sammy had come across on one of their mountain adventures a year earlier. This summer had been something of a disappointment because their parents had jointly issued a ruling that there would be no more overnights together for the two. "Not proper given your ages," his mother had announced. They could not travel far without an overnight stay or two—certainly not to this cave—but the parents had stood united and firm. A guy would think, their children being older, parents would loosen the reins on kids instead of tugging them tighter.

They still took day hikes on occasion and frequently worked together on wood cutting, gardening, and other projects. They were often business partners and had sold a fair number of melons, potatoes, and ear corn to Jeb

Oaks for his store and split the profits. Trouble had invited Sammy to join his trapping enterprise, but she had refused, declaring she wanted no part of killing innocent animals. Well, the buffalo robe she had sent with him had not come from a criminal. An animal had to die for that wolfskin coat that kept her so warm in winter. And the meat that valley folks ate almost every meal was not grown in a garden.

Trouble hoped his mother and the Morris family were unharmed and that his disappearance had not placed them in danger. Perhaps he should not have stopped off to tell Sammy what he was up to. He should have found a way to Mister Gains as soon as he escaped the killers. From his hideout in the steep rock wall that rose above a canyon rim, he had seen searchers still riding mountain trails. He supposed the sheriff's killers would have decided to let him be and moved on. But the deputy could not allow that. If Brady Yates survived, Ferd Bullock could very well end up dancing in the air with a noose about his neck. And there was the man in the suit. He did not look like a man who would thrive on the run.

He could not spend his life here, however, and he had decided that the next morning, he would take a chance and start his journey back to Lockwood. If he could get that far, he would hide till daylight and then walk right into the bank and Mister Gaines's office.

Beyond the cave's narrow mouth, it was nearly pitch black now at the rear of its almost eight-foot depth, signaling that the sun had dropped behind the mountains. Trouble had laid a small tipi of kindling on the cave's stone floor in the event he decided to risk a fire. He had finished the rationed bounty sent by Sammy in the first two days but had collected an armful of cattail shoots and roots, miner's lettuce, willow bark, and other edible plants. Most were best eaten in spring and early summer, but the inner willow bark seemed to know no season and he had gnawed the soft flesh off the tough outer layer. Most of the plants would have tasted better boiled and seasoned with sage, but uncooked they helped fill an empty, gnawing belly.

But he had snared and skinned two rabbits, and he craved meat. The coolness of the cave was holding off rancidness, but his harvest should be eaten soon. Before lighting the fire, Trouble went to the cave entrance and squeezed through the ragged, vertical slit that allowed access. It was too narrow for a bear, he figured, but a cougar could wedge through without difficulty. He stepped out onto the small rock outcropping that provided a landing on the steep mountainside to this place accessed only by a winding goat trail. The footing was treacherous, but he would not be taken by surprise here or swarmed over by a crowd. Unfortunately, in the event of attempted escape he would provide a snaillike moving target for any marksman from the riding trail that wound along the mountainside some sixty feet below.

He cast his eyes over the chasm below. A stumble here would send him tumbling down the steep slope to the trail below, bringing a rockslide with him. If he were lucky, he might roll to a stop on the trail. Otherwise, a few more feet would carry him over the edge of the canyon's rim where he would plummet in freefall as much as five hundred feet to the awaiting rock floor.

Low-hanging clouds blocked any starlight or moonglow, and the bite of a stiff breeze stung his cheeks. Nights had a way of bringing on a chill quickly in the low mountains, and he wondered if the clouds did not suggest snow in the peaks further west. He prayed not, for those snows could move down anytime when October arrived. He was grateful that the cave at least blocked the wind and mentally thanked Sammy again for insisting he take the old buffalo robe. He looked forward to wrapping himself in its warmth after he roasted and ate all he could of the rabbits. He had not slept much since retreating from the valley, but tonight he was ready to collapse.

The thought of rest evaporated, however, when he saw the flickering lights of campfires, blinking like fireflies in the trees below. Three of them, probably a mile or two between each, one in the canyon below, another on the far side. The one that worried him most was the one near the beginning of the trail that led up the mountainside in the direction of his hideout. But who was tending those fires? They could be trappers, but not likely all three. Trappers were fewer these days, and it was not prime trapping season. He had to assume that the fires belonged to searchers combing the mountain trails out of Lockwood looking for Trouble Yates.

It would be too dangerous for the men to move in the dark, especially if they were horse mounted, and somehow, he doubted if such men would walk anywhere that they could ride. The cave was not easily noticed above the trail. He and Sammy had found it accidentally when she was watching an eagle nesting in some gnarled trees jutting from the cliffs above the entrance, which at first appeared to be a crack in the stone from their range of view. If the pursuers were not experienced trackers, there was little chance they would find him here. Even if they found the goat and deer trail that angled up the slope away from the main trail, most would not detect human tracks on the shale and stones that formed the pathway.

He dared not leave the cave tonight, and even with the cover of the cave a fire would be unthinkable. Someone's eyes might pick up the sliver of light on the face of the mountainside. He slipped back into the cave, abandoning for the moment his thoughts of succulent roasted rabbit. He fell upon the buffalo robe and wrapped it about him, burrowing into the cocoon he formed. Sleep wasted no time claiming him.

# Chapter 11

IT WAS WELL after sunrise when Trouble awakened to the sound of voices outside the cave. He rolled out of the buffalo robe, snatched up his Winchester and crawled to the cave's entrance, taking care to keep his head away from the shard of sunlight that sliced through the opening. He raised himself on his knees and peered out. He saw a burly man standing on the trail below with the reins of a sorrel horse grasped in one hand. He could not make out the man's features from the angle and distance and with hat pulled low on his forehead, so he could not tell if he was anyone Trouble might know.

The man was looking in the direction of the cave opening, so his hideout had obviously been identified. But how?

The man called, "What's taking you so damn long, Nighthawk?"

Trouble thought there was something familiar about the voice.

Off to Trouble's right, a gruff voice replied, "Trail not for man. You want, I come down, and you drag fat ass up here."

"I don't see how he got up there if you can't make it."

"I can. But Trouble is little guy. Shut up, so can hear."

Nighthawk. Brule Sioux. Not like the others who had melted into the community and were welcomed as productive citizens. He had lost his wife and farm to demon whiskey. He was a big man with a gut, crowding fifty, Trouble guessed. Nighthawk was assumed by many folks to be rustling cattle and stealing anything he came across but clever enough not to get caught. It made sense that he would be a part of anything illegal that was going on in the North Laramie river valley and that they would recruit a Sioux tracker or two for a mountain hunt. How many were searching? How many Sioux? Not more than two or three. He knew all the Sioux and mixed blood families in the valley, traded with them regularly. After Sammy, his best friend was Running Fox, a Sioux boy his age and the adopted son of lawyer Ethan Ramsey and his half-blood wife, Skye. His friend's white name was Jacob Ramsey. He wished Jake were with him now.

Nighthawk yelled again to his comrade, "Tracks old. Maybe week. Betcha Trouble gone now."

"Got to look. If you ain't seen tracks going back, you need to see where he headed and stay on his trail."

Idiots. How did they think they would surprise him yelling back and forth like that? Or maybe they thought he was a defenseless kid and would give up without a fight. He knew this much. These men were not after him to hold for ransom someplace. They wanted him dead. He eased back into the depths of the cave, his eyes fixed on the opening, and propped himself up on one knee. He levered a cartridge into the Winchester's chamber.

He could hear the rattle of small stones and sliding shale outside. Nighthawk was nearing the entrance.

"Hey, Trouble. You in cave?" Nighthawk hollered.

Trouble did not reply.

"Come out. All okay. Take you home to mama."

"You think he's just going to come walking out of there and fall into your arms? A kid that's made it this far ain't likely going to make it easy. Get your ass in there and see if he's still around. Time's a wasting," the man on the trail below hollered.

"You come up, you no like how I do this," Nighthawk replied.

The cave turned darker as the Sioux moved in front of the opening, blocking the sunlight. Nighthawk thrust a hand holding a pistol into the entrance and followed with his head. Trouble could see the man's eyes darting as they tried to pick out some sign of his occupancy, but the Sioux would see nothing until his eyes adjusted to the darkness. Nighthawk said, "Trouble, you answer me. You there?"

Trouble squeezed the trigger and the rifle sounded like a dynamite blast as the shot echoed off the cave walls. Nighthawk's head jerked back from the slug's impact and Trouble planted another slug in his chest before the big Sioux dropped off the narrow trail and commenced his ride down the steep slope, bounced off the main trail, and catapulted into the canyon's depths.

Trouble moved to the opening, readying the rifle for a shot at the Sioux's companion. He looked out and saw that the man was struggling to hold his panicked mount. The horse had evidently been frightened by the gunshots and the rockslide that had carried Nighthawk's corpse past them. The man was an easy target, but knowing it was contrary to all good sense, he struggled with the thought of squeezing the trigger. But what would he do with a prisoner?

He watched while the horse calmed, and he knelt behind the scattering of stones on the ledge outside the cave's entrance, drawing a bead on his enemy while he waited. When the mount finally quieted, the man turned around and looked up toward the cave entrance.

"Unbuckle your gun belt and drop it," Trouble hollered. The man ducked and reached for the holstered gun. Trouble squeezed the trigger and got off a shot, but the gunman had hit the ground and Trouble could not get a decent angle for a shot without showing himself.

He pondered the dilemma. The outlaw's handgun would not be accurate at the distance between them, and his foe shared the awkward angle. Trouble did not have time to waste. Others would have heard the gunfire, but in this rugged country it would take time to reach him, possibly hours. However, their search could be narrowed and focused now. He stood up and saw the man flattened on the trail, his pistol raised and seeking its target. Trouble fired, aiming for the man's hip. A shriek followed by moans and a string of cussing told him he had hit his mark.

"Throw your gun over the rim of the canyon, or I'll fire a kill shot," Trouble warned.

"You will kill me anyway."

"I am not you. I will not," Trouble replied.

There were a few moments of silence before the pistol flew over the canyon's rim. "Stay put," Trouble said. "I'm coming down."

He reentered the cave and gathered up his buffalo robe and possible bag, slipping his arms through the shoulder loops on the robe and hooking the possible bag strap in the crook of his arm. He reluctantly abandoned the rabbit carcasses but stuffed an assortment of his plant harvest into the bag Sammy had given him and tied it to his belt. He was not going to be roasting rabbit any time soon and handling his rifle with the load he already had during the descent to the main trail would be all the challenge he could manage.

Trouble stepped out of the cave's entrance again and cast his eyes over the main trail. The man he had shot lay motionless in front of the sorrel. The horse tossed its head uneasily but was considerably calmer than it had been earlier. The trail was too narrow for the animal to turn around here and it could not back down the steep incline. Soon the sorrel would decide to bypass its owner and move on until the trail widened with an outcropping of rock or an acceptable destination was located. A showy animal, he thought, with a white mane and tail. From its size, and muscular ranginess, he did not think the horse was a mare. It could be a stallion, but more likely a gelded critter.

He started his trek slowly down the barely discernible path that snaked its way down the mountainside to the main trail. He hugged the rock wall, praying that his footing would not crumble away and launch him on a death ride. He tried to keep his eye on the gunman, who could still represent a threat, if he got to his feet and reached the rifle in the scabbard hanging from the horse's saddle. As Trouble approached the juncture of the trails, he lost sight of both man and horse, which made him uneasy.

As he stepped onto the main trail and made the turn west to head up the slope again, to the point below his former hideout, he tensed and readied his rifle. He did not like killing, but he knew now he could do it if the necessity was forced upon him in order to save his own life or that of someone he cared about. He relaxed when the sorrel and its fallen owner came in sight. The man was still down, and as he drew nearer Trouble wondered if he had died. When he came up behind the horse, he confirmed that the animal was gelded and every bit the prime specimen he had judged from a distance. He began talking softly to the horse, and the sorrel's ears pricked up, but he did not move away. Trouble stepped up beside the gelding, gently patting the horse's rump and slowly working his hand up to the muzzle. His other hand latched onto the reins.

He looked down at the gunman, who was lying face-down, breathing heavily and sobbing. "Hey, mister," he said, "roll over so I can see your face."

"I can't. I'm dying."

Trouble moved closer and studied the form at his feet. The man's left buttock was caked with blood. "You ain't dying. Not from this anyhow. I shot you in the ass. Now turn over."

The wounded man obeyed, but when he rolled over and leaned back against the stone wall of the mountain-side, Trouble learned that his target was more boy than man. Sixteen-year-old Butch Hugel, his nemesis—the bully who had endowed Trouble with his nickname. He looked up at Trouble with fearful blue eyes, his long, tangled brown hair covering a puffy face that could boast no more than a half dozen chin hairs for a beard.

Shaking off the surprise, Trouble said, "Well, Butch, we meet again. I haven't seen you since you left school a few years back. You're with the bunch that's trying to kill me?"

"Didn't want to. Just business. Working with my pa these days."

Jake Hugel was a no-account who was said to be a hired gun of sorts. About the only thing Butch and Trouble had in common were absent fathers. Butch's pa was always gone on undisclosed missions, likely criminal in nature, most thought. Of course, his own father had been thought dead until he showed up and surprised wife and son one day. "Who's paying you?" Trouble asked.

"Nobody knows. But you're worth a thousand-dollar bonus to the man that brings you in, dead or alive."

"And you were planning on collecting that reward. You and Nighthawk?"

"Nothing personal. I ain't got nothing against you. Just a job. Let me take you in and I'll split the reward with you. Won't cost me nothing since Nighthawk's dead."

"If I went in with you, I'd be dead, and you know it."

"I'd see that your ma got your share."

At least he wasn't denying the death sentence.

"Well, I've got to be moving on. I'm taking your horse with me."

"You ain't gonna kill me?" Relief spread over Butch's face.

"You're not worth wasting a bullet on."

"You ain't got a chance. There's at least ten out there looking for you. You're as good as dead."

"Then I'll see you in hell someday."

Trouble took the canteen that was suspended by a strap wrapped around the saddle horn and dropped it in front of Butch. "I suppose somebody will be coming this way soon enough. Hope they don't kill you."

"What do you mean?"

"They wouldn't want to answer questions if they took you to a doc for that ass wound. And you may know too much for your own good."

"My pa wouldn't let nobody kill me."

"I wouldn't bet one of my cats on his life, either. I don't know what the hell is going on, but I'm thinking you are both into something that will find you swinging from the end of a rope if somebody else doesn't take you down first."

Trouble tugged on the sorrel's reins, and the gelding did not resist as the horse stepped past its former owner and headed up the trail toward the high country.

# Chapter 12

DARBY STEPPED ONTO the boardwalk in front of the sheriff's office, walked up to the clapboard building, opened the sagging, squeaky door, and stepped inside. She found a middle-aged man, reminiscent of a scarecrow in build, leaning back in a chair with booted feet propped on a large desk. A smaller desk pushed up against a wall across the room was obviously for someone of lesser authority. The man had his thumbs hooked under bright blue suspenders and what appeared to be a new Stetson pulled down on his forehead. He was either snoozing or ignoring her. She suspected the latter.

She waited a few moments for acknowledgment and, receiving none, sat down in one of the two captain's chairs in front of the desk. She took her notebook and pencil from her bag, pushed her spectacles down her nose a bit and began writing. That appeared to get his attention, and he swung his legs off the desk and straightened in his chair. He pushed his hat back and glared at her with dark eyes. His narrow face carried several days of black stubble, and now her nose informed her he stank of sweat, horseshit, and booze.

"What are you doing?" he asked, nodding at the tablet in her hands.

"I'm making my notes about my impressions of this office, and I will make a record of whatever you have to say. Your badge says you are deputy sheriff. I have just noted I received no greeting or courtesy when I came in."

"I am Acting Sheriff Ferdinand Bullock. Who are you? Some newspaper reporter or something? I can't tell you nothing about the sheriff's and the whore's death. It's all confidential until the investigation's done."

Darby retorted, "And it appears you are very busy with that."

The sarcasm blew past Bullock. "It's a lot of work. In a week or so, we'll have something to tell the public. I can give you an invitation if you want. You didn't tell me who you are."

Darby plucked her Pinkerton badge and credentials from her bag and placed them on the desk. "My name is Darby Crockett. I am a contract detective with the Pinkerton National Detective Agency."

Bullock's face softened and Darby could see uneasiness replacing anger in the deputy's eyes. She wondered if his britches were wet. He looked over the badge and certificate and pushed the objects back to Darby who returned them to her bag.

Bullock said, "I never dealt with Pinkertons before. You're not the law, though. State your business. I ain't got time to waste on social talk."

"A man after my own heart. I don't have time for chitchat myself. Two colleagues and I are in Lockwood to investigate the deaths of Sheriff Will Bridges and Lucy Brisbane. We are also instructed to investigate the disappearance of a boy, one Brady Yates."

"Trouble Yates? Nobody's reported him missing. I don't know where you got that notion. And why would you want to check out Will's killing? You didn't waste no time getting here."

"Let's just say there are some important people interested in these cases. We are here to help you wherever we can and to conduct an independent investigation."

"Don't know what I'd need help for. Folks out this way don't take to having outsiders sticking their noses into things."

"Are you saying you won't cooperate with our investigation? We are certainly willing to share our findings with you. We could help each other, but that is entirely up to you."

"Well, I ain't saying I don't want to help. It's just that some things is confidential, and I got to be careful about what I let out to folks. I don't know much about Pinkertons, but you ain't official law. I know that much."

This was a man who had taken orders his entire life, Darby judged, and Ferd Bullock was struggling with the responsibility for decision-making on his own. She would bet he had a boss he was itching to rush to right now. If she did not loosen his mouth this afternoon, she likely would not have another opportunity. She decided to soften her tone.

"Look, Sheriff, I understand confidentiality. You have a lot of responsibility, and I am sure you are trying to do whatever is necessary to bring the killers to justice. What if I just ask you some questions, and if you are not comfortable with answering one, you just say 'confidential,' and I won't press you more on that subject?"

Bullock said, "Well, I suppose that would be all right. And you would share what you know with me?"

"Under the same rules."

Bullock asked, "Okay, who hired you?"

"Confidential. But I can tell you our orders came directly from the home office in Chicago. That tells you our client is somebody with important connections."

Bullock's eyes widened, and he wiped his brow with a ragged handkerchief. "My turn," she said. "Did Sheriff Bridges tell you he was going to visit Lucy Brisbane?"

"Well . . . uh . . . no. I mean a man like the sheriff wouldn't just say he was going to go meet up with a whore, would he?"

"That depends on the purpose of his visit. I will answer a question before you ask it. So far, our investigation indicates that it was highly unlikely the sheriff was making a visit for conjugal purposes."

"Visit for what?"

"For a sexual encounter."

The acting sheriff's face turned scarlet at the mention of sex. "Oh, well, I wouldn't know. Don't have no evidence one way or the other. But most folks assume Will was making a . . . a social call."

"But do you have any evidence of that?" Darby asked.

"No, I guess not. Do you have any evidence it wasn't?"

"No, I do not, but we are working on the assumption that he was visiting Lucy Brisbane as a part of a criminal investigation." The suggestion was total guess on Darby's part, but she wanted to test Bullock's reaction. His pale face and horrified eyes said it all. She was onto something.

"I guess you can assume what you want, but that don't make it evidence."

"It most certainly does not. But we find that the certain road to failure in a criminal investigation is to assume that the most obvious scenario is fact. We will look at all possibilities, as I am confident you will. May I ask what your theory of the murders is, sheriff?"

"Well, looks to me like Will did make a social call to Lucy's. I worked for Will a long time. He was still a randy old coot. Liked the ladies, and his wife had been gone a spell."

"How do you know this?"

"Just things he'd say sometimes. Told me once he thought he'd like to get acquainted with Lucy. I figure somebody Lucy had been taking care of come along and was jealous of the sheriff's being there. Decided to do them both in. Probably that simple."

"Who performed the autopsy on the bodies?"

Bullock hesitated. "Weren't none."

"No autopsies? Why not?"

"They was dead. What more did we need to know?"

"Who made the decision not to have autopsies?"

Again, Bullock stalled. Finally, he spoke, "I did, and I ain't got no more to say. Anything else is confidential."

Darby decided the man was engaged in a dance of lies and half-truths and that it would do no good to pursue the interview further. "Just one more question," she said, "Do you think Brady Yates's disappearance has anything to do with the murders?"

"Confidential," Bullock replied.

"I take that as a 'yes.' Do you know what I think?"

"I don't much care what you think, ma'am."

He was bristling now. She had touched a tender spot. "I'm going to tell you anyway. I think the boy you call 'Trouble' is real trouble for the killers. I think he saw something, and some people want him dead. I promise you this. If Brady Yates is killed, this valley will be swarming with Pinkerton agents, and they will be here until his killers are brought to justice."

Darby stood and turned toward the door. When she went outside, her eyes surveyed the business buildings that lined Main Street. She saw Oaks General Store, where the stagecoach had dropped them off, on the opposite side, and she stepped off the boardwalk onto the dusty street and headed for the establishment.

She entered the store, which seemed to be doing a brisk business and wandered about the premises, looking at the merchandise nearest the window and watching the sheriff's office as she wandered about the store. It was a roomy, well-stocked store, and she had not seen its equal in her hometown of Boston or during her other travels that included stopovers in St. Louis, Kansas City, and Denver. She promised herself to return to do some price comparisons before departing the community. As she had anticipated, Acting Sheriff Ferd Bullock soon emerged from his office, looked up and down the street.

Darby quickly slipped out the mercantile door just in time to see Bullock enter the Gaines Bank building. She had expected him to run immediately to the man he took his orders from, but surely that would not be Matthew Gaines. That made no sense. Gaines would not hire Pinkerton National Detective Agency to solve a crime he, himself, was involved in. Darby guessed she had misjudged Bullock's likely course of action. And yet, a seed of doubt was planted just before she was to visit some lawyers Gaines had assured her were totally trustworthy.

# Chapter 13

ENOS FLETCHER, THE proprietor of Fletcher's Livery was a wizened man with a face covered by a scraggly, obviously home-trimmed beard that was stained by tobacco and other substances of unknown origin. Deeply carved wrinkles fanned out from pale blue eyes that scrutinized the strangers who sought to rent some mounts for the afternoon. Trace noted that the man was a bit shorter than Maddie, but without the stoop and shrinkage of his years, he likely would have been at least several inches taller in his prime. Trace could not guess Fletcher's age, but it could be anywhere from seventy-five to ninety, he speculated.

"You want two horses, huh?" Fletcher asked, repeating what they had already told them.

"Yessir. We'll need saddles and tack. We've got scabbards for our rifles, as you can see."

"I don't hear so good, so you will have to speak up. And you got sort of an accent."

"I was raised in Tennessee."

"Confederates?"

"I was too young. My father fought for the South." The war had technically ended over seventeen years earlier, but Trace wondered if it would ever be over. He added on the chance it might make a difference, "I wore blue during the Red River War."

"Fought Comanches, huh?"

"Yes, now about the horses."

"You're a big feller. I got a tall, muscled gray gelding that should suit you. The young lady would match nice with a buckskin mare I got if she can handle a spirited critter."

Maddie spoke. "She sounds perfect."

"You can look them over. If you don't like my picks, you can check some of the others."

"We need some directions," Trace said. "Maybe you can help us."

Fletcher spat a wad of gooey tobacco at his feet, several drops catching on his already decorated beard and painting the left side of his lips. "Try your luck."

"Yates place?"

"Don't know if I should say. There's been problems out that way. Don't want no part of sending more to that nice Missus Yates."

Trace took his Pinkerton badge from his shirt pocket and held it out. "We're here to help Missus Yates."

"I can see a badge. Can't read what it says without my specs."

Trace said, "It says 'Pinkerton National Detective Agency.' We are Pinkerton detectives. We want to speak with Missus Yates and her neighbors."

"You going to find Trouble? That's her boy's handle. Think he's got another name but don't know it."

Evidently, Brady Yates's absence was community knowledge, although Trace suspected Enos Fletcher would be the first to know of any irregular occurrence. "Yes, we are going to try to locate Trouble."

"I sure as hell hope you do. He's promised to buy this place in three years if I can hold on. And I'm betting that kid will do it. Ain't never seen the likes of that one. He's a pistol, let me tell you. Always on the move. Only one in this town that makes me feel old. You know about the sheriff's killing? Him and Lucy Brisbane?"

"I do, as a matter of fact."

"Some say the sheriff was paying for pokes. Some cowhand didn't like him laying with Lucy. That's pure bullshit. I come to this town before Will Bridges even. Knowed him twenty years. Good Lord ain't made many better than Will. He picked up his horse here that day. Told me he was going to have a talk with a witness. Didn't say who, but when I heard they was kilt, I figured Lucy was the witness. Don't take but a dab of brains to figure out Trouble Yates knows something about it."

"Do you have any idea what kind of a case Miss Brisbane might have been a potential witness in?"

"Can't say for sure, but Will had been worrying about killings of two miners five months or so back. They was scalped to make it look like Indians done it but ain't no Indian troubles around here since Custer met his maker. Will said it weren't no Sioux scalping—more like a hog butcher's doings, he said."

"Is there gold mining in the Laramie Mountains?" Trace asked.

"Folks look for it; silver, too. But none found that I know of. But these fellers had digging gear with their pack animals. But he was even more upset about killings of a nice ranch couple a few months back. Frank and Cora Woods. Had a place north and west of the river, not far from the Laramie foothills."

"Any strangers in town?"

"You and your lady friends. Folks are mighty curious about who you might be. But there have been others, too. More gunslingers than I seen since the bloody range wars a few years back. Two or three suit types in and out of here last summer. A couple smelled like government. One strutted like money. Will asked me what I knowed about them, and I told him what I'm telling you. My gut says they was men up to no good. Didn't do no business here."

Trace asked, "Did you tell the deputy or anybody else about this?"

"Nope. I've lived a good long life, but I'd like to live a mite longer. Man's got to be careful who he tells what, and Ferd Bullock would be the last I'd speak to about anything."

"You don't think much of Bullock, I gather."

"The most dangerous people are them that is either stupid or evil. Ferd, he's both."

Trace decided he would speak to Enos Fletcher again. The man was feeding him teasers, testing him a bit. Fletcher knew more, perhaps more than the old geezer realized.

# Chapter 14

TRACE HAD LOOKED over the available horses at Fletcher's Livery and found he could not dispute the owner's selection of mounts. Fletcher had provided simple directions to the Yates and Morris farms, as well as to the house that Lucy Brisbane had rented, which was an easy stop along the route to the others.

They reined their horses into a long, winding lane bordered by oak and pine that led to the Brisbane house. The big wolfdog followed behind, leaping off the road from time to time to sniff whatever interested him and to deposit several drops of piss if he deemed it worthy. Trace wondered if the creature ever ran dry. Soon they came to the house, a whitewashed, clapboard cottage in a clearing surrounded by the woodlands.

"I love this setting," Maddie said. "It's so calm here. The little stable off to the back wouldn't hold more than two horses, but that's enough. There's a water pump just outside the stable besides the one just a few steps off the porch. Convenient."

Trace said, "You don't mind being away from people, do you?"

"Not as long as I've got Pirate and a rifle or shotgun."

They dismounted in front of the house and hitched their mounts to a rail there.

"What are we looking for?" Maddie asked, as she followed Trace on his meandering route around the house, skirting the fringe of the forest.

Trace stopped when he saw what he was looking for. "Something like this." He pointed to an opening in the woods where a horse's hooves had broken into the soft earth. Evidence of horses breaking through the forest and undergrowth was revealed by intermittent bent and broken limbs of trees and shrubs and mashed leaves and grass.

Trace said, "A horse went through here, probably two. I'd say the riders were looking for somebody."

"Like Trouble Yates?" Maddie asked.

"Could be." He turned away and headed back toward the house.

As they went up the porch steps, Maddie nodded at the plank floor. "That's blood, isn't it?"

Brownish black stains nearly covered the area just outside the door. "Yeah, appears like it."

"Looks like a steer slaughtering."

"Matt Gaines said that the sheriff was riddled with bullets."

"More than one shooter, don't you think?"

"Seems likely."

He checked the door. No chain or padlock outside. He turned the handle. "Not locked," he said.

Trace stepped inside and cast his eyes about the parlor before waving Maddie in. The room was freshly painted a pale blue and apparently was well kept except for the signs of the obvious struggle that had taken place here, evidenced by chairs overturned and a broken kerosene lamp on the floor. The lamp triggered the thought that it was strange the killers had not pulled the sheriff inside and burned the place down. They could have charred the bodies beyond recognition and cast considerable doubt on what happened there. Perhaps, they were interrupted by something. Awareness of an observer? Of course, among the criminal class there was a severe shortage of high functioning brains.

He walked into the only bedroom. Like the parlor, it had been torn apart, and otherwise would have been quite welcoming with its bright yellow walls and flowered curtains. He guessed that should have been no surprise, the deceased being in the business that she was. The sheets and blankets on the bed had been blood soaked and were now stained beyond rehabilitation. Strangely, nobody had bothered to clean the house yet, but Gaines had said it was a rented place on his lawyer's land, so it might have been left undisturbed so the property could be inspected by legal authorities if they chose. Given the property's history, there was likely no need to rush in preparing it for a tenant.

Out of the corners of his eyes Trace glimpsed Maddie bending and retrieving an object from the floor. He continued pacing about the room. It was a west room with two windows providing ample, early afternoon sunlight. He had decided there was nothing in the room that would shed light on the case when Maddie spoke.

"Trace, look at this." She extended her hand palm upward and showed him a turquoise stone about a half inch in diameter.

"From a pendant?" he asked. "Or a bracelet?"

"I couldn't say. There is a crust on the bottom that tells me it was set in something, probably silver. We should find out if Lucy Brisbane was wearing a bracelet or jewelry when they found the body. I looked in the drawers of her dresser and came across a tarnished silver bracelet, and a gold cross pendant, of all things. Several sets of simple earrings. Strange, isn't it, a lady doing what she did for a living having a cross pendant?"

He took the polished stone and shoved it in his pocket. "I suspect it gave her comfort. I'm not a religious scholar, but I recall that the Good Book warns us not to judge others lest we be judged. My dad always cautioned me not to judge another man until you have walked a mile in his moccasins. Different ways of saying the same thing, I guess. By the accounts we have picked up so far, most folks around Lockwood didn't think ill of Lucy, and it appears she was a good citizen. I wonder if that's how she got mixed up with something that cost her life?"

# Chapter 15

WHEN TRACE AND Maddie came to a sharp bend in the river trail that signaled nearness of the Yates house, Trace said, "Enos Fletcher said the house should be less than a quarter mile after we make this turn. I'm not going to visit Sarah Yates just yet. Thought I would have a chat with the fellow who is watching her place first. Why don't you cross the river here? You can go on ahead and talk with Samantha Morris. There is a shallow off to your right where the river has filled in some with shale and sand. According to Fletcher, stay with the river and you will end up at the Morris house."

"I can do that. Do you want Pirate to go with you?" Maddie said.

"No, keep him with you. After you talk with the Morris girl, hold off crossing to the Yates farm until you hear me fire three shots just seconds apart. Don't pay attention to any other shooting. Wait for the three successive. You got a timepiece?"

"My grandfather's pocket watch in my saddlebags."

He plucked his own watch from his trouser pocket and checked the time. "Not quite two o'clock yet. If you have finished talking to Samantha Morris and don't get the signal by three-thirty, hightail it back to town and meet up with Darby."

Maddie squinted one eye and looked at him quizzically. "You don't listen to your wife very well, do you?"

"Oh, I listen well enough. I just don't always take her advice. Now, I need you to get moving. I'm thinking the lookout might spot you and keep his eyes on you while I try to work my way around the farmstead. Matthew Gaines said there is a wooded knoll beyond and behind the barn some distance, and that's where the lookout has been spotted several times. He apparently doesn't make much effort to conceal himself."

Maddie said, "So I'm a decoy of sorts."

Trace thought a moment, "Yeah, I guess maybe you are."

"Just wondered." She reined her buckskin mare toward the river, and Pirate fell in behind.

Trace dismounted and, taking the reins of the gray gelding, started his walk in the opposite direction. As he moved away from the river, however, he found the woodlands thinning, and soon he came upon shortgrass prairie that had attracted ranching interests to the Laramie valley. His movement would be easily detected by an observer on high ground. He surveyed the vast landscape and caught sight of what appeared to be a gap in the terrain to the north. Remaining under cover of the forest, he angled in that direction and came to a deep ravine that cut across the prairie and disappeared behind the hill where he hoped to find the guard. The passageway would not render him invisible to a watcher's eyes, but it would require some focus for someone to pick up his movement once he crossed the thirty or forty feet distance to the ravine's edge. Regardless, the lookout could not be certain of Trace's destination or whether he was a threat to his assignment.

When he reached the ravine, Trace was pleased to find that its depth was no more than ten feet and that the sides sloped gradually to the bottom. He led the gelding down one of the crisscrossing deer paths and continued his journey along the rocky trail below. As he neared the knoll overlooking the Yates farmstead, he caught sight of a bay gelding staked out in the grass at the foot of the hill, confirming the accuracy of his guess about the location of the lookout. He led his mount out of the ravine and onto the flat and staked the gelding within a stone's throw of the bay. Then he began a stealthy climb up the slope.

Halfway up the incline, a scratchy voice from off to his right said, "Looking for somebody? And don't go for your gun or you are a dead man."

Trace gambled. "Ferd sent me out to call you in."

A wiry man of medium height stepped out from behind a pine tree. He was dressed in black from head to toe. A low-crowned, planter's hat was set low on the forehead of a weaselly face, and he moved with an effeminate grace, Trace thought. He clutched a pistol in his right hand, pulled from an empty, jeweled holster on his right hip. Another holstered pistol was at the ready on his left. There was no doubt that this pretty man fancied himself an elite gunslinger. And he possibly was, considering he appeared to be a few years past thirty and still alive.

"Ferd sent you?" the man asked. "The halfwit deputy?"

"Yeah. He said to tell you to come in. They got the kid."

"That don't ring true somehow. Ferd don't give orders. He takes them. Did he tell you my name?"

"No. I didn't ask. He just told me you would be at the Yates place and you would be wearing black."

"Seems strange he didn't give you my name. I go by 'Slick.' What's your handle?"

"My name is Trace Crockett."

"Crockett. Related to Davy?"

"Distant cousin."

"Sure you are. And if your name is Crockett, I'm Abe Lincoln."

"Glad to meet you, Abe."

"Smart mouth is a good way to get a chunk of lead between your eyes."

Trace said nothing.

"Now, tell me what your real business is here. Ferd wouldn't be sending any orders. Any word would have come direct from Weaver. Besides, I ain't seen you at any of the Laramie Rider gatherings. If you're a new rider, convince me."

Slick had not lowered his pistol an inch, and it was aimed at Trace's gut. Trace decided the truth was no more dangerous than a lie. "I am a detective with the Pinkerton National Detective Agency. I have been called in to investigate the killings of Sheriff Will Bridges and Lucy Brisbane." In case this did not work out well, he did not want to disclose the presence of other agents in the area.

"And what were you planning to do about me?" Slick asked.

"I intended to ask you to leave this place and stop harassing Missus Yates with your presence. You are a trespasser. Mount up and ride out, and I'm done with you unless we meet up again."

Slick laughed, and Trace dropped to the ground and rolled just as the gunslinger's pistol fired. He had his Army Colt in his hand before he stopped, scrambled to his knees and squeezed the trigger, he felt the burning of Slick's second shot tearing through his left shoulder at the same instant that his Colt's slug burrowed into the gunman's gut.

Slick looked down at the blood leaking through his shirt and then glared back at Trace with disbelief in his eyes. "You son-of-a-bitch," he said. He started to raise his gun for another shot but slumped and tumbled forward before Trace could fire his own weapon again.

Trace got to his feet and holstered his Colt, then tentatively ran his fingertips over the bleeding shoulder wound. It appeared to be a pass-through shot that had entered and exited the thick muscle high in his shoulder. It was not life-threatening if he could stem the blood flow. He ripped off the remainder of the shirtsleeve below the partially shredded shoulder fabric, and, feeling nauseous and dizzy, sat down, leaning against a tree trunk while he fashioned a crude compress to hold against the wound.

Then he remembered. Three shots. He drew his Colt and aimed it skyward, squeezing the trigger three times.

# Chapter 16

MADDIE AND SAMANTHA Morris sat on the porch steps of the Morris's log house. The most important information Maddie had gleaned was the disclosure of a cave where Brady Yates might have gone for refuge. Samantha also spoke of other routes Brady might have taken deeper into the mountains.

"If you search for Brady, you must take me with you. I know almost every place he might have gone. I've hiked and camped those mountains with him."

"What would your parents think about that?"

"You've met them. They'll worry, but they'll give in to the idea, knowing I would be with Pinkerton agents and that I might help find Brady."

"It makes sense, but I need to get approval from Trace and Darby Crockett. They are my bosses. I'm a new agent."

"How did you become an agent? You can't be more than sixteen or seventeen years old. I'm thirteen."

"Actually, I am fifteen going on sixteen. It's a long story, but I am sort of on probation right now. You might say I have to prove myself."

"You must like doing detective work. It sounds exciting."

"It is fascinating." The wolfdog sat just off the steps beside her and she reached out and scratched his ears. "Pirate likes the work. But he has got to prove what he can do, too. He was caged up in a little pen when we lived in Kansas City with my father. I won't let that happen again, no matter what."

"He's a beautiful creature but strange looking. His eyes would be scary if you met up with him alone in the woods."

"He's at least half wolf. He found me in a place called 'No Man's Land' near Indian Territory. He saved my life by leading me to the cabin where he and his owner had lived. I found the owner's remains there and buried him. After that, I stayed on until the Pinkertons found me."

"How did you come to be at such a place?"

Maddie started to explain and then the gunshots echoed through the river valley. "I will tell you about it another time," she said. "I'm heading for the Yates place. Those shots could mean Trace has a problem, or they might not. I'm supposed to wait, but I've got to find out."

"I'll go with you. I'll show you the crossing, and I can introduce you to Sarah Yates. I don't need to saddle my horse. Since I'm wearing my britches, I can run beside you and cross on the footbridge. I love to run."

After they crossed the river, they moved along a wide cleared trail through the woods that fringed the river. When the Yates house came within sight, they heard three rapid gunshots.

"That's the signal. That means Trace is okay."

As they reached the house, another gunshot cracked, the sound clearly coming from the knoll above the farmstead. Maddie said, "I don't know what that means. Pirate and I are going to take a look. Why don't you tell Missus Yates about our visit, and I'll be back with Trace shortly?"

"Okay. Behind the barn, ride to the edge of the tree line. You will pick up a trail that takes you to the top of the hill."

"Thanks. I shouldn't be long."

Maddie got a glimpse of the attractive blonde woman stepping out of the house to greet Samantha and gave her a tentative wave before reining the buckskin toward the barn. She easily found a well-used trail that snaked up the slope and through the trees and brush. "Find Trace, Pirate," Maddie said. She had no illusions that the dog understood anything beyond her permission to take off on his own, but the huge dog bounced ahead of her and soon disappeared into the trees.

Moments later, Maddie heard the wolfdog barking frantically. She nudged her mount forward, picking up the pace until they reached the hilltop. Part way down the other side she saw Trace leaning against a tree, his head sagging against his chest and his left shoulder and shirt-front blood-soaked. Folded fabric torn from his shirt-sleeve lay in his lap, where he had apparently dropped it. She dismounted, hitched her horse to a low-hanging pine branch, and rushed to his side.

Avoiding the black-clad body laid out some twenty feet distant, she hurried to Trace's side, yelling, "Trace. Trace."

She knelt beside him, and his eyes opened. "Hi, Mad," he said. "I hoped you would figure out I needed some help."

"Thank God," she said, "I thought you were dead. Tell me what to do."

"Take some cartridges from my gun belt and load my Colt."

"I can do that, but why?"

"I'll explain later."

With trembling fingers, she worked cartridges out of the belt and pressed them into the revolver's cylinder. She laid the grip of the weapon in Trace's right hand. "Now what?"

"The two horses are staked out in the meadow on the backside of the knoll. You need to get them up here so we can load the body on one and get me in the saddle on the other. I'll be okay. Bleeding's down to a trickle if I don't move. May need some more patchwork before I mount my horse, though."

"I can help," came the voice from behind Maddie.

She started and whirled around. "Sammy. I thought you were with Missus Yates."

"I explained that some Pinkerton agents were here to find Brady and that I would be right back. Seemed to me that if your friend was signaling for help, you might need another hand."

"You are right about that, young lady," Trace said. "You must be Brady's friend, Samantha Morris. I'm Trace Crockett, and I thank you for coming. I'll be all right here if you two want to get the horses. But take your Winchester with you, Maddie, just in case. Get back here fast if you spot anybody."

"What do you mean?"

"They were watching the house twenty-four hours a day, I assume. One man couldn't do that, so they must have had one or two more keeping a lookout in shifts."

"Pirate will warn us," Maddie said.

Suddenly, a loud growling and snarling from downslope turned their heads. It was followed by a man's anguished screaming and cursing, then sobbing. "Sammy stay with Trace," Maddie ordered.

Maddie yanked her Winchester from its scabbard, levered a cartridge into the chamber and ran toward the sound. The woods had quieted now except for the man's crying and sniveling. Not far downslope, Maddie came upon a young man with shoulder-length hair stretched out on the ground, his bloody wrist locked in Pirate's teeth, his six-gun lying on a bed of oak leaves well out of reach.

Maddie leveled the rifle at him. "Okay, mister. I can shoot this Winchester better than any man or woman I know. And I've killed before. Didn't bother me a bit. Make a move for your gun, and you're dead."

"Whatever you say, ma'am. Just get this creature off me. I'm all chewed up. Please, you won't get no trouble from me, I swear."

"You try, and my wolfdog will finish you off. Pirate, release."

The dog opened his jaws, and the young man withdrew a mangled hand and wrist. Maddie figured he wouldn't be able to hold a gun in his hands for days, might even carry some permanent damage. The other blood-covered hand and arms appeared to have fared only slightly better. "Stay put," she said, and while Pirate stood by his adversary emitting a low growl, she stepped over and picked up the dropped pistol and a battered hat that clung to some brush.

"Can you walk?" she asked.

"If I can get to my feet." He rolled over, groaning as he pressed his bloody hands to the earth, raised himself to his knees, and stumbled to his feet. She gestured with her rifle barrel toward the hilltop where Trace and Samantha waited.

When they reached Maddie's companions, she saw that Samantha had removed the dead gunslinger's shirt and was salvaging the unbloodied part for compresses and bandages. She appeared unfazed by the unpleasant task and was deftly fashioning a wrap that covered

Trace's shoulder wound and bound his upper left arm to his chest.

When Maddie walked back into the little clearing, Trace looked at her with disbelief. "A prisoner?" he said.

"Unless he gives us a good reason why he shouldn't be," she replied.

Trace said, "Sammy, why don't you see what you can do for this man's hands and arms? After that, maybe you gals can go bring back some horses while I have a discussion with this young man."

Maddie said, "Okay, but Pirate stays with you."

# Chapter 17

TRACE REMAINED SITTING on the ground with his back supported by the tree and the wolfdog sitting a few feet away. He was feeling noticeably stronger now, and his grip on the Colt was firm. The prisoner sat on a flattop stone some ten feet in front of him, forearms and hands wrapped, so they were virtually useless. He could not be more than eighteen or nineteen, Trace guessed. Time enough to turn his life around if he had not done anything yet to put a noose around his neck.

The kid needed a haircut and a shave, although the beard was so sparse, plucking would be easy enough. Tall, skinny guy with light blue eyes that betrayed his fear.

Trace asked, "What's your name, kid?"

"Roscoe. I'm hurting. I need a doc," he moaned.

Trace figured pressing for a last name would be a waste of time. Odds of the response being truthful would be poor and irrelevant in any event. "A doctor will come see you at the jail."

"Jail? I ain't done nothing."

Trace nodded toward the dead gunman. "Slick there said enough to start you on your first step to a noose around your neck."

"What do you mean? I ain't done nothing. I was just looking around the place."

"That makes you a trespasser. But Slick said a fella named Roscoe was coming to take over his watch," Trace lied. "That means you are one of the Laramie Riders."

"That ain't no crime."

Trace gambled. "The Laramie Riders murdered the sheriff and a young woman."

"That was Slick's doing. The woman, anyhow. Another guy that was there told me."

"So you do know about the killings?"

"I said all I'm going to say, mister. I don't even know who you are."

"My name is Trace Crockett. I am a detective for the Pinkerton Agency. We've been brought in to find a missing boy—the boy you've been watching for—and to bring the sheriff's killers to justice. You can stew about that while you sit in the county jail. You might think about talking some to save your own hide. If you weren't in on the killings, you've still got a chance at a fresh start on the right side of the law."

"I didn't know there was any killing on this job. Thought I was working for the government. You put me in the jail, and I'm as good as dead."

"Why is that?"

"The deputy. He's in on it somehow. He'll see I don't stay alive to talk."

"The deputy was in on the killings?"

"I don't know if he kilt anybody, but he was there. That's what Slick said."

"Who else was there?"

"I don't know. Slick was liquored up when he was bragging about it. Said he'd kill me if I said a word. Guess that ain't going to happen. Damn, I'm hurtin'. I need sewed up and something to help the pain."

"We'll both visit the Doctor when we get to town, and if you agree to help us, we'll try to find a place to put you for safekeeping."

"I got to think about this."

Trace had his own hurting to deal with and found himself nodding off again. "Roscoe," he said, "I'm going to nap a spell. You make a wrong move, and Pirate here will finish you for dinner. You understand that?"

"Yessir, I do. Don't want no problems with that critter. Ain't in no shape to do nothing anyhow."

Trace dozed off until he heard Maddie and Samantha talking as they led the horses through the trees and brush to the top of the knoll. They appeared shortly with Samantha leading his gray gelding and Maddie leading Slick's black horse and a blue roan gelding that had to be Roscoe's.

He nodded at Roscoe, "At least you're a fair judge of horse flesh."

"Damn right I am. I know horses."

"You won't be seeing any where you're headed."

Roscoe just scowled.

Maddie asked, "Are we taking the corpse with us?"

"We are if we can throw him across his horse. Then Roscoe and I will have to ride. Suppose you ladies can double up on your buckskin?"

"Sure," Maddy said, "but Sammy can outrun any of the horses down the trail."

Roscoe's disabled hands and arms rendered him useless in lifting the body onto the horse. Fortunately, Slick was not a big man, and with the assistance of Trace's good arm and shoulder, Maddie and Samantha were able to slide the corpse over his horse's back and then anchor it with a tether rope.

"Did you notice," Maddie asked Trace.

"Notice what?"

"The holster. Slick's left holster is decorated with turquoise stones imbedded in silver settings. One stone is missing. I would bet the one in your pocket fits perfectly."

# Chapter 18

D ARBY SAT IN the conference room of the Ramsey and Locke law firm. A pert young woman with copper colored hair and greenish-blue eyes sat across the table from her. Hannah Locke was the firm's junior partner, pleasant enough but a bit reserved, perhaps wary. Darby placed Locke at about her own age, a few years past twenty-five.

"I suggested we meet here," Locke said, "because I knew that a Pinkerton agent referred by Matthew Gaines would be someone my partner, Ethan Ramsey, would want to speak with. He and Matt are close friends and share concerns about the community."

"I'm curious," Darby said. "I have worked with a lawyer in Manhattan, Kansas, where my husband and I currently live. Myles Locke. He practices with his son. I don't suppose you are related."

Her reply was terse. "He is my father. We are estranged. I haven't seen him for eight years. He writes. I don't."

That was clearly the end of their conversation about Myles Locke. Darby could not resist saying, "My parents live in Boston. We are estranged, too. I write. They don't."

Hannah Locke could not hide the surprise in her eyes, and the two women froze in an awkward silence for several moments. Darby was relieved when a distinguished-looking man in his mid to late thirties opened the door and entered the room. He reminded Darby of her own husband, tall and lean, impeccably dressed in a gray pinstriped suit. He stepped immediately toward Darby and she stood and offered her hand. His warm smile softened her before he took her hand in a firm, but not crushing, grip. "I'm Ethan Ramsey, and please call me Ethan. Sit down, please, Miss Crockett. I'm sorry, or is it Missus?"

"Missus Crockett, but I'm more comfortable with 'Darby.'"

Ramsey sat down, taking the chair beside hers. "Matt Gaines told me he was contacting the Pinkerton Agency. Suffice it to say that I am Matt's personal lawyer, and I know about all his concerns. Tell me how I can help."

Darby took that to mean that Ramsey knew about Gaines' relationship to Brady Yates and that it was likely that Miss Locke did not. Most lawyers knew where the bodies were buried but kept their mouths shut. She assumed Miss Locke would be informed only if it became pertinent to the firm's legal business.

Darby said, "Our priority is to find Brady Yates, and the two other detectives, one of whom is my husband, Trace, and I will be heading out to search for him tomorrow. I'm concerned that we don't even know where to start looking. Trace and our associate, Maddie Sanford, are talking to some folks who may be able to help."

Ramsey said, "Call on me if I can be helpful. I don't know that you require a tracker, but I was a scout out of Fort Laramie during the Sioux and Cheyenne Indian wars. My wife and I operate a ranch, and I still spend a fair amount of time in the saddle. I was handling a legal matter in Cheyenne when Will was killed and just got back a few days ago, or I would have hit the trail with a few of my Sioux friends. But Matt had left word for me to speak to him as soon as I got back, and he told me that Pinkerton agents were due to arrive."

This soft-spoken man was obviously a person of many dimensions, one who could be genuinely helpful, Darby surmised. There was something about his manner that invited trust. She decided to ride with her instincts. "As I am sure Mister Gaines told you, we have also been employed to investigate the killings of the sheriff and young woman."

"Yes, he did. Will Bridges was a good friend of mine, and I want to see justice done. Of course, finding Brady Yates might go a long way toward solving that case. By the way, I should tell you that our ranch company owns the cottage where the killings took place. We bought it with a quarter section from a farmer who moved on, and it's several miles from our operations, so it has usually been rented out to somebody. Lucy always kept it up better than anybody who has ever lived there."

"What is your opinion of the deputy, Ferd Bullock?" Darby asked.

"I think the county board made a mistake appointing Ferd acting sheriff. It was a quick and easy way to fill the vacancy, but Ferd is lazy and has a dim candle burning in his brain. Bad combination."

Darby said, "I spoke with him at the sheriff's office before I came here. I don't think there is a chance he will solve the case or even try. He's someone else's puppet, and I think he's in over his head."

"That wouldn't surprise me," Ramsey said.

"After I left his office, I stepped into the general store across the street and watched the sheriff's office for a spell. As I suspected, Bullock went out the door. I assumed he was on his way to the puppeteer."

"And was he?"

"He entered the bank."

Ramsey's impassive face told her nothing.

"Why would he go to the bank?" she asked.

"Perhaps he was simply depositing or withdrawing money."

"Or he was reporting to his boss." Darby said.

"You're not suggesting that Matt is somehow involved?"

"It makes no sense. He's providing the funds for the investigation."

"I'll vouch for Matt's integrity. Of course, you don't know me well enough to be assured I can be trusted."

"I trust both you and Matt Gaines. You are right. Bullock must have been doing some routine banking."

Hannah Locke, who had been a silent participant to this point, spoke. "Craig Hammer."

Darby turned toward Hannah. "Who is Craig Hammer?"

Hannah replied, "Vice president of the Gaines Bank. My former fiancée."

"I see." She did not, but thought under the circumstances it would be better to let the lawyer lead the conversation.

Hannah continued, "I'm just mentioning Craig as a possibility. If money is a motive in whatever is going on, Craig should not be stricken from any suspect list. I know I must sound like a woman scorned, but I am the one who broke off our engagement last January after investing over a year in our relationship. He is not an honest man."

"Does he hold any ownership interest in the bank?"

"No. He is an employee and unhappy that Matt has declined to sell him any stock. I don't think his job is secure. He is a smart man who can be very charming when he chooses, but at the time of our split he had already used information acquired at the bank to purchase a few small properties. He bragged about it to me, and that's when our engagement started to unravel fast. The remainder of our sick story is irrelevant."

Darby could see no reason to press for details about the aborted romance. Most people carried secrets they were reluctant to spill out to other ears, but she did want to know more about Craig Hammer. "Can you think of any reason why Hammer would be mastermind of a plot to kill Sheriff Bridges?"

"Not a mastermind, but if it was necessary to save his own skin, it would not be beyond him to participate. With Craig, it would be something done in a moment of panic or a task carried out at someone else's orders. And I don't see him pulling the trigger. I'm a ranch girl, and I can use a rifle or pistol. Craig's a city boy from New York. He was horrified to learn that the venison I was serving him came from a buck I shot. He carries a derringer in a little belt holster at the small of his back. It's hidden under his waistcoat, but he would probably shoot himself in the foot if he tried to use it."

Darby said, "I might want to ask you more about him. I'm not ready to have a chat with him. I need to know more first, and, again, Brady Yates is our priority."

"One thing I almost forgot," Hannah said. "I was in the deed recorder's office last week searching title records on some land a client was planning to buy, and I came across some purchases Craig had made. Three parcels. Eight hundred plus acres altogether. Worthless woodlands in the foothills as near as I could figure. Adjacent to government lands. Land in that area isn't farmable even after it's cleared. Rocky slopes. Not worth clearing to shift to grass."

Darby said, "You're talking my husband's language, but I get the point. Why would a banker be buying land like that?"

Ramsey said, "Unless he's already figured out how to make a profit." He was quiet a moment. "I have had several clients tell me about contacts by someone claiming to be an agent for an anonymous land buyer. You know ranchers and farmers, though. They marry the land when they buy it. They don't divorce casually."

"Something to ponder," Darby said.

They talked for another half hour, exchanging theories about the motives for the killings and Darby garnering information about the Laramie valley and Lockwood in particular. Hannah Locke seemed more at ease as they talked and even surrendered an occasional smile.

As she readied to depart, Darby thought of something else. "Bullock said there was no autopsy made of the bodies. That seems very strange in a case like this."

Ramsey said, "Not in small counties in these parts unless the sheriff orders it.

The county prosecutor can override the sheriff's decision, but that's Logan Wyatt, and he wouldn't order anything done unless family members or somebody insists on it. Will had no family. I will be executor of his will when it is probated. I know Logan well enough that I could have pressed him on it, but the bodies were buried before I got back. Logan's carrying a lot of years on his shoulders, and the prosecutor's job is just part-time, as needed here. Pays a little of nothing."

"Who performs the autopsies?"

"Doctor Henry Weintraub. He's the town's only physician. Good man. Very skilled. We're lucky to have someone of his education and abilities out here in isolated mountain country like this."

"Would the undertaker be able to tell us much about the injuries?"

"That would be George Caldwell. He runs a little tavern that caters to folks who don't want to mingle with cowhands and day laborers. Undertaking is just a sideline. He has a back entrance for that business." He smiled. "Tavern is called 'Dead Man's Paradise.' I have spoken with him. He said Lucy's face and body were badly bruised, but she was killed by a single bullet in the temple. Powder burns suggested the gun was fired up close—like an execution. Her body was discovered unclothed."

"What about the sheriff?"

"He had been shot at least six times, twice in the head, the others in the torso. Sounds like more than one man took him down."

"Do you know who found the bodies?"

"Jimmy Tate. A young cowhand not more than twenty. Works for the Bar X, a big outfit. Speculation is he was a potential customer stopping by Lucy's for a . . . visit. Anyway, to his credit, he rode into town to report what he found."

"Okay. I appreciate your help, both of you. I hope my associates find out enough this afternoon that we can put some of the puzzle together." She got up to leave, and the others joined her.

As they stepped into the outer office, Ramsey said, "Darby, I've been thinking. If you and your colleagues wouldn't mind, I would like to ride along with you tomorrow. I know this country, and I don't think I would be a burden."

Darby turned to Ramsey and replied, "Given your background, I would hardly see you as a burden. I can speak for my colleagues. Yes, you are more than welcome to ride with us. Seven o'clock tomorrow morning at Fletcher's Livery."

# Chapter 19

TROUBLE YATES RODE Butch Hugel's sorrel gelding deeper into the high country, leaving a sobbing Butch on the trail behind. He felt a twinge of guilt at leaving his former schoolmate there fearful for his life, reminding himself that Butch had been on a mission to kill him. Regardless, he hoped that Butch was not further harmed or even killed by his fellow hunters. He guessed that the would-be killer would be taken to somebody higher up the chain who would decide the boy's fate. Perhaps the father would be able to talk the son free from the dilemma.

He looked skyward and calculated that he had six to seven hours of daylight. The sorrel appeared to be a sure-footed critter and showed no signs of nervousness with an unfamiliar rider. Trouble did not mind getting off his own feet a spell and the spot he had in mind for his next stop would shelter a horse and offer a little grazing and water. What worried him most were the ominous gray clouds dropping below the mountain peaks to the west. For now, he would savor the warmth of sunshine toasting his back.

He needed to change course tomorrow and take a horseshoe route back out of the mountains. If he could slip into Lockwood at night and get to Fletcher's Livery, he was confident old Enos would hide him and help him arrange contact with Mister Gaines. He did not know Ethan Ramsey so well, but Ramsey was his mother's lawyer and had helped Trouble with collecting a bill from a deadbeat cat buyer at no charge. He would ask Enos to contact Ramsey if Mister Gaines was not available. Looking back, he should have circled back to town the moment he abandoned Abner and the cart that day. All he had thought about then was running far and fast.

He urged his mount up the trail that widened for a spell, allowing him to move ahead faster. On the other hand, pursuers would have the same advantage. When he reached an escarpment that allowed him to ease off the trail, Trouble dismounted and climbed upon a mound of stones overlooking the trail and canyons below. The overview of the winding trail was obscured at many points by ragged stone walls, and initially he saw no sign of fol-lowers. He started to turn away when he saw a flash of light on the trail some distance below. Sun rays glancing off metal. He waited and watched, and three riders came into view. Not far away as the crow flies, but a few hours maneuvering the twists and turns of a steep trail. But he was not certain he could make it to his intended destination without leaving sign before they closed the gap, certainly not with the sorrel.

He forged ahead until the landscape leveled off onto a plateau-like shelf carpeted with mountain grasses that he knew from past visits extended for several miles and offered prime grazing for deer, elk and goats. He could move his mount ahead at a faster pace, but the searchers would have the same benefit. As he approached his destination, he looked over the trees and undergrowth that shrouded his potential hideout and decided he would be forced to abandon the horse he was becoming fond of. He could not slip through the aspen and pine leading the sorrel without leaving obvious signs.

There was a route up a steep, stone incline that would allow him to circle around and come out above the unfinished, abandoned mine shaft dug into the mountainside, but a horse would be unable to negotiate the rocky wall which was nearly vertical in places. Any doubt regarding his decision was removed when huge snowflakes began drifting downward like floating goose down from a sky that was still partially sunny. This told him that the sun would disappear soon and that low-hanging clouds would be dumping a fair amount of the white stuff by nightfall.

Trouble dismounted and gathered up his gear and removed the gelding's saddle bags, figuring they might come in handy later. The bags were not heavy, so he did not bother to empty them, thinking he would check them out when he got settled in someplace. He removed the horse's saddle and bit and bridle and tossed them over the edge of a shallow ravine where they were unlikely to be noticed and would doubtlessly be snow covered within an hour. He marked the spot mentally in case he had an opportunity to salvage the tack later. They would be worth money, and Butch Hugel would not dare lay claim. He held out some hope that he might yet recover the horse, but he slapped the animal on the rump, sending it down the meadow a short distance before the gelding stopped and turned, looking back at him wistfully.

Trouble headed into the rocks, hoping the sorrel would move on and not mark the place of his exit. The horse would be fine. This early snow would be an inconvenience but would not be life threatening to the animal, which would eventually make its way down one of several trails that led back to the valley, where there would be little, if any, snowfall.

Trouble loved rock climbing and the trek over the stone-sheathed slope of the mountainside would have been easy for him without his rifle and gear, but he had to move slowly and cautiously along the wall using hand and footholds he and Sammy had speculated might have been carved by ancient mountain occupants. The wall started to slope noticeably as he neared the shaft, and by the time he reached a dip in the incline, he was able to slide to the clearing below, taking several nasty bumps and gouges on his journey to the ground.

Trouble clambered to his feet and looked about, taking a quick inventory of his surroundings. He figured he was nearly a hundred yards from the trail he had just departed and positioned on low ground below the sightline of any searchers. Besides, he enjoyed the shield of thickly forested ground between the mine and the trail. He still hated surrendering the sorrel, though, for there was a rough wagon road from this place that wound down the mountainside and eventually angled in the direction of Lockwood. He supposed there was some risk that one of his pursuers might cross the trail someplace and follow it for ease of travel. But when he and Sammy had come across the mine more than a year ago, the wagon path was nearly covered with knee-high pine and shrubs taking root in the rocky soil and so deeply rutted it would not likely offer an invitation to most travelers.

A narrow stream rushed over a rocky bed nearby, and crude stone fortifications had been constructed by the aspiring miners near the entrance to the mine opening. Enos Fletcher had told him that there were many aspiring miners working the hills in the late forties and early fifties, dropouts from their journeys to the great California gold rush. A short-lived gold strike in the westernmost part of the territory had spurred the fever in Wyoming for a spell, but it had died quickly, and the fortune seekers had moved on. Enos said the move had been encouraged by the Sioux who had taken more than a few scalps to make the visitors feel unwelcome.

The falling snow was starting to lay a thin white blanket over the ground now, so he headed up the rise to where the mine shaft was located. When he reached the opening, he was surprised to find that all the boulders that had offered cover to the miners from warring Sioux or claim jumpers had been cleared away. He stepped inside the entrance a few feet, his eyes searching the dark interior for bears or other creatures that might greet him with fury. He heard nothing, and when his eyes adjusted to the darkness, he could find nothing threatening for as far as he could see in the gray gloom that gave way to total blackness.

As he recalled, the excavation had been more cave than shaft when he and Sammy explored, its depth being no more than twenty feet. It seemed deeper now somehow, but it could not have changed in that short time. There were other such excavations scattered about the area. He had been told that the government owned the land on which the undeveloped mines were located as it did most of the mountain country in the territory. Much of the foothills and the portions of the valley that were publicly owned were leased to ranchers or farmers who had no economic use for the high country.

Trouble thought he would like to own some of the land up here. It would be perfect for lumbering if he owned a sawmill, but transporting the harvest could be a challenge. Worst case, his acquisition could be used as a private retreat someday. When he got out of the current mess, he decided he would talk to Mister Gaines or Mister Ramsey about how a person would go about buying government land. Of course, such a purchase was several years distant.

Nightfall was just a few hours away, and the billowing clouds that were dumping the snow had now successfully blocked any warmth he might have gathered from the sun. He was more hungry than cold, but he was not going to locate food sources until the snow let up. He spread out the buffalo robe far enough back from the entrance to escape any wind. He tossed Butch's saddlebags on the robe and sat down Indian-style to rummage through the contents, not expecting to find the treasures that were secreted there.

He opened one side of the bag and found a sheathed Bowie knife. He removed it and unsheathed the blade. Nice for show, he thought, and probably worth some money. Not practical as a skinning knife or tool for frequent use. He was more enthused when he came across supper and breakfast—a handful of deer jerky strips, three hardtack biscuits and a small paper bag of mixed hard candies, including peppermints, lemon drops and cat's eyes. Digging deeper, he also discovered a few grimy, coiled licorice ropes stuck to the bottom of the compartment. Of course, Butch would have kept a supply of snacking edibles within reach, and he would have required food during the search. Butch would not have lasted long on what he had, though. Trouble guessed the riders had not intended to be out long on their search or returned to some base camp to resupply when necessary. They were showing no signs of giving up the chase.

Trouble opened the flap on the other side, and his eyes widened when his fingers worked through some dirty socks and underwear and felt a cluster of flat, round-shaped metal objects. He clutched his hand about the discovery and plucked them out. His eyes widened in disbelief when he opened his hand and saw the double eagle gold coins. Five of them. One hundred dollars. He stuffed the coins in his front pocket and searched the saddlebags again to be sure he had not missed any other treasures.

Then his conscience started nagging. Did he have any right to claim the coins? He figured they were a down payment on his own life, and he was confident Butch would have killed him in an instant given the opportunity, especially if Trouble turned his back to a readied weapon.

He would think on it, maybe seek out Mister Gaines's advice. His mentor had told him more than once that folks had a bad habit of deciding they wanted something and then digging up all the reasons they could think of why they should be entitled to it. They sometimes chased this thing even if they had to do something illegal or immoral to get what they desired. He had called it "helpful rationalization." Outright thieves did this, convincing themselves they were somehow entitled, Mister Gaines had said. He had even admitted that he was ashamed to say he had given in to helpful rationalization more than once. But it haunted him when he did. And he enjoyed no peace till he set things right. "Nothing's worth it," the banker had admonished.

Trouble ate one of the jerky sticks and a biscuit and then popped a peppermint in his mouth and walked downhill to the stream and filled his canteen. His growling stomach told him that the small bit he had eaten just whetted the appetite, but until he found another food source, he should ration what little he had. The deepening snow made this especially important.

Later, fighting off the temptation to build a fire, Trouble lay on the stone floor of the mine shaft rolled up in the buffalo robe, thanking Sammy silently for insisting that he take the mangy thing with him. He was nodding off to sleep when he heard something or someone crashing through the trees and brush to the south, the direction of the trail he had abandoned just hours earlier. He scrambled out of the warm robe and pulled on and tied his clodhoppers. Then he snatched up his rifle, levered a cartridge into the chamber and stepped to the mine opening, edging off to the north side and hugging the wall. The snowfall had not eased, and he could see little through its white curtain. He watched intently in the direction of the noise that was coming slowly but steadily toward him. He could not judge the distance of the approaching man or beast, but the source of the racket was not far from his hiding place. He raised the Winchester to his shoulder and waited.

# Chapter 20

I T WAS AFTER sundown when Trace arrived at Fletcher's Livery with his bizarre caravan. He was surprised to find Enos Fletcher on duty, having assumed that the old man would have a stable hand to handle night hours. Fletcher came to the front of the stable, cocked his head to one side and scratched his whiskers.

"Didn't expect you would be working this late," Trace said, wincing at the pain that had started to shoot through his shoulder intermittently since they left the Yates house and headed along the river trail to Lockwood.

"I got a room I live in at the back. Don't have to hire much help that way. I thought you was just going out to have a little chat with some folks. If this is how you do your talking, I think I'll just keep my mouth shut if you don't mind."

"Can you direct me to the doctor's office?"

"Hate to tell you, but the doc ain't going to help the feller tied down on the horse's back." He looked at Samantha who sat behind Maddie astride the rented mare. "Sammy, why don't you show these folks the way to Doc Weintraub's and roust him out." He reached for the reins of the dead man's horse. "I'll take this feller down to Dead Man's Paradise and tell George he's got a customer, but I ain't standing for the bill."

"Tell the undertaker that I'll pay for his services, and that he should talk to me before the man is buried." Pinkertons would probably frown when they saw burial costs on the expense account, but Trace did not much care.

"I'll tell him just to store the corpse till you show up."

Trace asked, "By the way, have you ever seen this guy around?"

"Yep. Left that same horse here a few times but ain't seen him for a spell. Thought he'd left these parts. Showed up alone. Unfriendly sort. Had a sour look that would pucker a hog's ass. Strutted like a gunfighter. I'm sure he killed a fair number in his time, but I'd bet most was backshot."

"Any idea where he went from here?"

"Yep. I notice things. He always went to 'The Doll House.' Just down the street from here. Walk out to the middle of the street and you can see the place. It's the big barn-looking building on the side street off Main about a half block west. The entire premises take up five times what my business does, and part of it is two stories."

"Interesting name. What kind of business is this Doll House?"

"Excuse me, ladies. Plug your ears if you want."

Trace noticed that his companions were more attentive now.

Fletcher continued. "It's a drinking and whoring business. Drinks on the main floor. Women on the second floor. Come to think of it, Lucy Brisbane worked there when she first came to town. But that was three or four years back. She left after six months or so and set up her own shop. Big fuss about her going and she got the hell beat out of her before Will Bridges stepped in and warned them off."

"Warned who off?" Trace asked.

"Reggie Weaver and his thugs. Reggie owns The Doll House. Always has three or four no-goods around. They quiet things down when it gets too rowdy or if some feller is getting rough with a woman. Understand now, I ain't never been inside the place. Just telling what I've heard."

"Well, I thank you for the information. I guess we had better be moving on." He turned to Maddie. "I'm feeling dizzy again, Maddie. I'll just hang on tight and you and Samantha lead the way."

# Chapter 21

THE LAST THING Trace remembered was riding away from the livery. When he opened his eyes, he was lying on a white-sheeted bed in an unfamiliar room. He turned his head and saw that he had a roommate stretched out on a bed no more than five feet away. Roscoe. The young man Pirate had nearly eaten for supper. His deep breathing and snoring signaled that he was in deep slumber.

A brew of the odors of medicines and anesthetics, including chloroform, filled the air and told him he was in the hospital. Trace was wearing a cotton gown, someone having absconded with his clothes, and he slipped his hand beneath it to test the wounded shoulder that was throbbing enough to make him aware of the injury, but the pain was not intolerable. He found the wound dressed and tightly bound.

He heard the swish of skirts and he looked to see Darby in the doorway. She entered, followed by a tall, white-coated man Trace guessed to be in his mid-thirties. He, like Darby, wore wire-rimmed spectacles and had a bookish look. Darby moved to his bedside and bent over and kissed him on the lips. "I love you," she whispered, before stepping back. "Trace, this is Doctor Henry Weintraub. You and I need to talk, but I will let Doctor Weintraub explain what he has done for you."

"Good evening, Trace," Weintraub said. "You are looking much better than when we first met. Enos Fletcher brought you to my door in a buckboard. He said you were leaving the livery and just dropped out of your saddle. Enos and your young friends helped get you inside and on the table. My wife, Ruth, assisted with the chloroform and dressing—she doubles as my nurse—and I cleaned the wound and stitched it, leaving a little gap so it could drain. As you probably know, the slug passed through the flesh. Your shoulder should be fine, absent any putrefaction, of course."

"Thank you, doctor. When can I leave?"

"Your wife said you would be asking that and told me that if you could get to your feet, I wouldn't be able to hold you anyway. I don't think you will be walking far without help this evening. Why don't you stay overnight?

We'll see how you are feeling in the morning. Ruth or I will be checking on you and Roscoe every few hours. See the rope hanging down from the ceiling next to your bed. Give that a tug if you need to use the chamber pot under the bed or any other assistance. A bell rings in our bedroom, and one of us will be here quickly. Any questions?"

"Not now, I guess."

"Very well." He turned to Darby. "He is all yours, Darby. Stay as long as you wish."

"Thank you, doctor. I will leave him so he can rest as soon as we discuss some business."

Doctor Weintraub smiled as he walked out of the room. "I think you have a grip on his reins for the moment, ma'am. Better take advantage of it."

Darby sat down on a stool at his bedside and looked down at him, her dark brown eyes glistening with tears.

"What?" he asked.

"You had me worried sick when you didn't get back before sundown. And then Maddie came into Sally's and called me out in the middle of supper. I knew something terrible had happened. Damn it, Trace," she said, "can't I let you go off on your own without you running into trouble? And I'm not talking about Brady Yates."

"Unavoidable," he lied. "But it was a worthwhile trip."

"It's never worthwhile if you come back slung over the back of a horse."

"But I didn't."

She surrendered a deep sigh. "I'm riding out in the morning with Maddie and Samantha to start the search for Brady Yates."

"I'll be fine to go in the morning."

"No, you will not. Do you want to risk somebody else's life if we're having to look after you?"

He knew she was right. He likely would not be able to sit in a saddle for any serious time. "But you don't know what you're going to run into. You've got two kids to back you if you run into gunplay in the mountains."

"I've taken on another man who knows what he's doing."

"Another man? Who?"

"A lawyer."

"I can't imagine what you would need a law wrangler for in the mountains."

"The lawyer is Ethan Ramsey, the man Matt Gaines suggested we talk to. He was a scout for the Army at Fort Laramie during the Indian wars. Chief of scouts, I have learned. I visited with Enos Fletcher after he hauled you here in the wagon last night. The Sioux called Ramsey 'the Puma' for his silent stalking ability. Enos thinks very highly of him."

"Okay, I'll feel better knowing you've got some help. And you will have the wolfdog. Did Maddie tell you that we got one of Brady's dirty shirts from Missus Yates. Maddie claims the dog can track by scent. I don't doubt it. I just know the creature may have saved our lives when my roommate was sneaking up on us. How is Roscoe doing, anyway?"

"He won't be a threat to anyone for a spell. Doctor Weintraub spent more time with him than he did with you. He had to take off the young man's trigger finger, assuming he's right-handed. It was just hanging on. Lost the tip of his little finger on the same hand. Left hand is all stitched up, but he should have normal function in that eventually. Won't know how crippled the right will be for a month or two."

"It's too bad, but Pirate might have saved him from a noose waiting in his future. Maybe he will have second thoughts about where he was going with his life." He thought a moment. "It just occurred to me. What are we going to do with him? From what the man, Slick, said, it seems likely that Deputy Bullock had some role in the sheriff's killing. I can't turn this young man over to the acting sheriff. He would probably be set up for an escape and killed."

"So, what do you do with him?" Darby asked.

"Keep him here for now. Return my guns, which I suspect you have stashed someplace, and I will stay with him until I can make other arrangements. I'll see if Doctor Weintraub can get word to Matt Gaines that I am here and need to talk with him."

"I have a feeling the good doctor is not going to be pleased about using his hospital for a jail. This big house serves as a six-bed hospital with three patient rooms besides his office, examination and surgery rooms, and he and his wife and two small children occupy the remainder of the house as their residence. He will not want any gunplay here."

"That's why I need to talk to Matt. I want to vacate this place before the day is done tomorrow."

"When you talk to Matt, warn him to watch out for the vice-president at his bank. His name is Hammer, and he is on the suspect list of those who might be involved in a conspiracy that included the killings," Darby said. "I will explain everything when we return. Hannah Locke at the Ramsey law firm can tell you about the conversation we had there."

"I'll warn Matt to watch his back. I don't want him to accidentally drop a clue to any plan."

"You've got something in mind. What is it?"

"I'm still in the thinking stage. You've got to get ready for riding out tomorrow. I'll be fine here."

"Is that a dismissal?" Darby asked.

"I'm tired, love, and you've got work to do. You can kiss me again before you go, though. But that's as far as you can go. We're on a business trip, you know."

"Since when has that mattered to you?" She stepped off the stool, leaned over the bed and pressed her lips to his.

# Chapter 22

THE BRUSH AND trees continued to snap as something—or someone—continued to crash through the woods toward the abandoned mine. Trouble half expected a grizzly or some other mountain monster to emerge from the trees at any moment. A man stalking him would be unlikely to make such a racket.

The noise suddenly ceased, so the visitor had either stopped or emerged from the forest. With the darkness and the snow dropping a white curtain in front of him, it was nearly impossible to see anything. His grip tightened on the rifle. Then he saw a huge, shadowy form approaching. It nickered softly, as it moved up the gentle incline to the mine. The sorrel gelding that he had turned loose.

Trouble lowered his rifle and waited while the horse came directly to him, whinnying with apparent recognition of its former rider. Trouble reached out and gently rubbed the horse's soft nose. The gelding was dusted with snow. The shaft's ceiling was too low for the visitor's comfort, and he figured it would spook the critter if he tried to urge it into the confining space. It seemed glad enough for company, and the shelter of the cliff wall would fend off some of the chill. Trouble guessed that the temperature was not many degrees below freezing and that sunshine would quickly shrink away most of the snow if it did not get much colder.

"Well, fellow," Trouble said, "I guess we're meant to be. I don't know how you found me here. I should have just brought you with me in the first place. Then I'd have a saddle. I can ride bareback well enough, but I don't know if I can handle you without a bit and bridle." He remembered that he had a coil of braided rawhide cord in his possible bag. Maybe he could fashion a halter and reins from that. Many horses neck reined, and he would see if the horse would react to the pressure of reins against its neck.

"Well, you are an old tagalong, fella. Think I will just call you 'Tag.' That be okay?" The sorrel nickered, and Trouble took that for approval.

It appeared the horse was going to stick around, and Trouble decided the mount would be something of a watchman. It was likely the sorrel would stir or whinny if anyone approached the mine opening. His main concern was the trail made by the horse. The snow would likely cover tracks, but it would not take an experienced tracker to observe signs of the gelding breaking through the woods. There were probably clusters of horseshit along the route as well. He hoped the pursuers had passed the entry spot by now and that the snow was rendering any signs of the gelding's passage invisible for the present. He had to force himself to care, he was so tired. He laid the rifle down next to the robe and burrowed in again, dropping to sleep quickly.

Trouble rolled out of the buffalo robe the next morning just before sunrise, relieved to find that the sorrel, Tag, remained outside the mine entrance. The snow had ended, too, and narrow fingers of sunlight reaching for the sky in the east suggested that the thaw he had hoped for would arrive by late morning. He breakfasted on another hardtack biscuit and strip of jerky and then cut a length of rawhide cord and quickly fashioned a rope halter for the unresisting horse. It was simply a matter of some loops and knots that he had done many times. A few more lengths for reins to tie to the halter, and he still had plenty of cord for a ten-foot lead rope and would have twice that left over. He feared that Tag might be more risk than help in eluding the men who were after him, but it seemed likely the sorrel was going to follow him regardless. Besides, they had bonded now, and he would not desert the horse a second time.

He led Tag down to the stream to drink, noting that the six-inch snow was already slickening from surface thaw. After the gelding drank its fill, Trouble took him downslope less than a hundred feet to a clearing where a fair carpet of grass lay under the snow. He cleared the snow from a small area with his feet to prove to Tag that breakfast lay there. The horse took the hint and began grazing. Trouble unhitched the lead rope, confident that his companion would not wander far.

He went back to the mine, sat down on a flattop boulder and took some time to ponder his situation. He quickly discarded the notion of staying over at the mine. He had spent nearly a week in the cave only a half day's hike from the river valley, thinking the chase might be abandoned, and then he could make his way to Lockwood without risk. He faced the reality now that he was not going to outwait the men looking for him.

He could not make sense of it all. Butch Hugel and his father, Jake, had not been present at the sheriff's killing. They had obviously been hired for the search, but why? Somebody else would have to figure that out. He just knew that he could not run forever. He must work his way back to Lockwood. He would head down the mine trail and keep an eye out. At the first sign of a searcher headed his way, he would slip into the woods, perhaps find a cross-trail. He might be forced to go higher into the mountains for a time but only for the purpose of picking up a route that led him to Lockwood.

His reverie was interrupted by voices, a man yelling for other men, and others more distant yelling back. Somebody had found Tag's trail. He leaped to his feet, quickly rolled up the robe, picked up his rifle and gear and raced to the gelding. He used his braided rope to secure his gear on the horse's back just above the flanks, so there would be room for him to slip in front if a riding situation presented itself. Then he started leading Tag down the old mine trail, noticing for the first time that someone had smoothed and widened it some since his last visit. Strange.

# Chapter 23

DARBY BROUGHT UP the rear of the mounted search party that rode out of the river valley and into the foothills at the base of the mountains. Ethan Ramsey led the riders, Samantha followed Ramsey, and Maddie tailed the girl with her big wolfdog ranging back and forth along the sides of the riders.

Samantha was leading the party to a cave she thought Brady Yates might have claimed as a hideout. When they approached a trail that wound into the mountains along a steep drop-off that would become an abyss as they climbed, Darby was half glad that Trace had stayed behind. The only thing he hated more than snakes was heights. He would have gritted his teeth and made the trek, but he would have been near panic every inch of the climb. She hoped Maddie did not suffer Trace's fear of heights. Samantha had obviously made the journey before and seemed unconcerned about what lay ahead. Ramsey signaled a halt, and they all reined in their mounts and followed his lead when he dismounted.

Ramsey walked over to Darby and said, "Ma'am, this is your parade. Sammy says the trail just ahead is the one that passes by the cave. It will take us to high country but it's firm and plenty wide for horses."

Darby turned to Samantha. "How near the trail is the cave, Sammy?"

"It's a ways above. More than fifty feet I'd guess. Maybe seventy-five. There is a foot path that cuts off to the cave from the main trail. It's kind of scary, but if you slip, you should just slide down to the main trail. Brady did that once and scared me to death. I thought he was going to topple off into the canyon."

"How long will it take us to get there?" Darby asked.

"Hard to say. I think it took Brady and me a good three hours to hike it."

Ramsey interjected, "The horses won't be galloping up that trail. Timewise, it should be some faster but not a lot."

Samantha said, "Sooner the better. I just want to find Brady and get him back home. I'm worried to death for him, and I'm mad at him for taking off like that. Does that make sense?"

Darby smiled and said, "It makes perfect sense, dear. I'm married to a man who does that to me all the time." She spoke to Ramsey. "We continue on in the same order. When we find this cave, we can decide how to approach things."

Ramsey pointed to the mountain peaks to the west. "It's been snowing up there. Storm appears to be over, but we might run into some on the ground higher up. The sun will have most of it cleaned up before the day's out."

It was late morning when Samantha informed them that they were approaching the cave site. Darby's heart raced when she saw vultures, the black harbingers of death, circling in the azure sky above the trail ahead, sweeping and diving to be replaced by others with slow, flapping wings lifting themselves from the landing place to join their comrades in the sky.

"Oh no," Samantha said, her words a near whisper. "Buzzards. Something's dead up there. Oh, dear God."

Darby knew that everyone was thinking it could be Brady, but no one dared voice it. What if their mission turned out to be a recovery one, where they would return to Lockwood with the body of this boy they were seeking? Your imagination is running wild, she told herself.

Ramsey signaled a halt and dismounted. "Wait here," he said. "I want to check ahead on the trail." He dropped the reins of his Appaloosa gelding, spoke softly to the horse that stood in place, and walked up the trail. She lost sight of the lawyer when he went around a bend in the trail. She saw vultures raise like a black swarm into the sky. It was only minutes but seemed like hours before Ramsey returned grim-faced.

"First," Ramsey said, "it's not Brady. But it's an older boy. I've seen him around town, but I don't know his name. I'm going to take a blanket from my bedroll and wrap him up. Later, Sammy, I'd like to see if you can identify him."

Samantha shook her head slowly and said, "I'll try." She pointed off to her left. "That's the trail to the cave. Shall I call for Brady?"

"It's worth a try," Darby said.

"Brady, Brady," Samantha called. "It's Sammy. Brady. I'm with friends who have come to help you."

No answer.

She called several more times to no avail. "I'll go up to the cave and see if he's there," Samantha said.

Darby said, "Maddie, if you can hold the horses, I'll go with Sammy."

Maddie took Brady's shirt from her saddlebags and held it out for Pirate to smell. "Take Pirate with you. He will bark if Brady has been in the cave."

Samantha moved up the narrow path like a mountain goat, the wolfdog at her heels. Darby lagged twenty paces behind, nervous about the tricky footing on the steep slope. Sammy called several times for Brady as she rushed toward the cave's entrance before the girl and Pirate disappeared inside. Soon Darby heard the wolfdog's loud barking. When she entered the cave, Pirate went silent and looked at her expectantly. She scratched the wolfdog's ears and cast her eyes about the dusky enclosure.

Samantha said, "Pirate's right. Brady was here." The dog was sniffing at the rabbit carcasses abandoned by Trouble and looked up at the girl. "I don't see why not." She turned to Darby. "He wants the rabbits."

"He needs to eat, and he might not have time to hunt."

Samantha said, "Go ahead boy."

Apparently understanding, Pirate tore his powerful teeth into the soft flesh of one of the rabbits and started his snack.

Samantha pointed to the remnants of cattails and other plants scattered on the floor. "These are things Brady gathered for a meal. When we hiked, we never took much food. He read constantly about wild plants and the things that could be done with them, especially how they could be used for food and medicines. He also talked to the Sioux when he could about such things. They didn't taste terrible when you got used to the idea. As good as some garden vegetables I have eaten. Brady likes to learn and experiment. Papa always says that Brady's a true free spirit, whatever that means. He even roasted some grass-hoppers and ate some one time. I drew the line there, and he was kind of disappointed in me, but I didn't care."

"We know he was here. The questions are how long, and where did he go?"

Samantha said, "I think he came directly here when he left our place. It was getting later in the afternoon when I saw him. It would have been dark by the time he got here. I can't think of any place that he could have gone that would be any nearer."

"That makes sense, and you obviously had things right when you said he would come here," Darby said. "And the food he left behind indicates he left in a hurry but had planned to stay for a time."

"Yes. He couldn't have carried all this with him," Samantha said.

# Chapter 24

SAMANTHA WALKED UP to the blanket-wrapped body with some apprehension. She had seen dead folks before at funerals on occasion after the undertaker had done his work and dressed the deceased man or woman in church-going clothes, but she had never seen a body in this state.

Ramsey knelt beside the body. "Sammy, I'm not going to lie to you. This will not be a pretty sight. This young man has a bullet hole in his forehead, and a vulture took one of his eyeballs. There is some skin torn from his face by the scavengers. You look, and tell me when you have seen enough, and I will cover his face."

She nodded. "Go ahead."

Ramsey pulled the blanket back, and Samantha instantly choked, fighting back vomit. She turned away. "Enough," she said. She could not imagine a more horrifying sight. The hole in the head, the empty eye socket and shredded flesh. Poor Butch. She had never been fond of him. A bully and smart mouth, but nobody deserved this.

Darby slipped past the horses and put an arm around Samantha's shoulders. "Sammy, you recognized him, didn't you?"

"Butch Hugel. Almost three years older than Brady and me. He tried to bully Brady at school till Brady bloodied his nose a time or two. Then he backed off. He dropped out of school a few years ago, and I would see him around once in a while, but never talked more than a 'hello.'"

"Jake Hugel's son?" Ramsey asked.

"That sounds right," Samantha replied.

"Jake's worked just outside the law for a long time. He could be involved in this and recruited his son."

Samantha asked, "You don't think Brady did this?"

"I don't know. There was a hip wound, likely a rifle shot from some distance that would have taken him down. The head shot was up close like somebody just pressed a pistol to his head."

"Brady would never kill anybody unless he was forced to. He just wouldn't. He would not have it in him to kill somebody in cold blood."

Ramsey looked at Maddie. "Could you and Sammy ride double for a spell, Maddie?"

"Sure. We did that on the way back to Lockwood yesterday."

"We might all have to walk some," Ramsey said, "but I can't bring myself to leave the boy here. We will strap him on Sammy's mount and then bury the body when we find a suitable place. If Brady's alive, it is safe to assume he headed deeper into the mountains, where he could get off the trail. I've never taken this trail, but I've been above here where the ground levels off some before the next climb. Some meadows the deer and goats love, not to mention horses that show up with riders on occasion."

Samantha was offended by the mere suggestion that Brady could be dead. "Brady's not dead," she snapped.

Ramsey said, "I didn't mean to upset you, Sammy. I am just saying we don't know what happened here. There is no way to tell if somebody dropped over the rim. We need to be prepared for any possibility."

Samantha said, "You saw Butch. He carries too much weight to have hiked this far. It wouldn't have been his way anyhow. Brady's got Butch's horse."

"I won't argue that point. We saw signs of other horses on our way up, more than one I'd say, given the piles of road apples we passed over."

Samantha tried to recall her trips up to the cave with Brady. "We never walked back down this way. We went up for another hour or more before it leveled out, and there are all kinds of ways back to the valley from there. Rough ground, but nothing as scary as the way we've come. We always figured that's why we didn't see signs that folks ever used the cave. A hard climb to get that far, and then it was set so far above the main trail. No place to graze horses here, so unless you were afoot, you wouldn't be staying overnight in the cave."

Darby said, "We had better get this poor boy's body on the horse and move on. Sammy, do you think an hour will take us off this trail?"

"Hard to say. We always walked, so we might do better once we get started again."

"Hopefully, we'll pick up some sign, but in case we don't, you be thinking about where Brady's next stop might be."

"I already have. The mine."

# Chapter 25

WHEN THEY RODE off the mountain trail and onto the meadow, Darby, although not an expert tracker, could see that there had been others ahead of them. Ramsey had already dismounted when she reined her horse over the rise. The ground was softer here and patches of the grass were matted down from hoof prints. She watched silently while Ramsey knelt and studied the ground and then got up and moved to another spot and did the same.

Finally, the scout-lawyer stepped over to her and said, "Four horses, I think, but there is a single set of tracks several feet out from the others that were probably made yesterday. The other three sets go alongside those hoof-prints, so they are probably following that horse. I am guessing they were made early this morning, but there should be some sign they camped up here on the flat last night. Nobody with an ounce of brain would come up this mountain trail at night. We've got to bury this boy and then we'll look around."

"How about over here," Samantha called. She and Maddie had veered off to the left while Ramsey and Darby remained near the trail.

Darby dismounted and led her bay gelding and the mare that carried the body toward Samantha and Maddie. Ramsey followed with his Appaloosa.

Samantha stood by a cluster of big stones, and when Darby approached, she said, "There's a washout here just before water drops down the mountain slope, but Papa would say it's not a natural watercourse. We don't have a shovel, but you could lay Butch in the hole and then cover it with a mound of rocks."

Ramsey said, "The body would be less than two feet below the surface, but if we could fill it with small stones and then build it up with some of the boulders, I think it would work fine."

Samantha added, "And it would be easy enough for family to find if somebody wanted to claim and move the body. Otherwise, Brady and I will make a grave marker and bring it up and place it someday."

What a special young lady, Darby thought. Her faith in Brady and trust that he would be found alive and well was unwavering. And whatever Butch Hugel may have done was forgiven, and she was determined that his last resting place would be proper and not soon forgotten. A world full of Sammy Morrises would be a much better place.

Everyone chipped in to fill the grave with stones, but Ramsey had to do the heavy work with the boulders. He did so without complaint, and she was surprised at his strength. He had not been exaggerating when he told her he was a working rancher, and he was thus a man accustomed to physical labor.

When the burial was completed, Samantha asked that they all stand together at the gravesite. Then the girl spoke, "Lord, we leave Butch Hugel to your care. I don't know how he felt about religion, but I doubt he ever had much teaching or a chance to learn of your Word. Please think of him as one of those who never had a real choice in the roads he took and take him into your arms like the forgiving God that you are. We entrust him to your care and mercy. Now, I ask everyone to join me in reciting the Lord's Prayer. Our Father . . . ."

It was the first time Darby had recited the prayer since she left Boston. She had been raised a devout Roman Catholic, but she had partially blamed the church for her parents turning on her when she humiliated the family with the prospect that she would become an un-wed mother. Then she had endured the miscarriage and been accused by her father of aborting the baby. There had been no winning in her dilemma, but there had been no reason to blame whatever God governed the universe. And the message of forgiveness was as much common sense as religious doctrine. It was like this moment was the first step of a journey to an unknown destination.

After the burial, they split up and started a search for a campsite where the mystery riders might have spent the night. No more than fifteen minutes passed before Pirate started barking and Maddie called for the others.

Ramsey seemed absorbed with something else and continued leading his Appaloosa along the edge of a wooded area north of the meadow. When Darby reached Maddie and the wolfdog, she confirmed that they had found the place where three riders had made a cold camp. Grass was matted down where three bedrolls had been spread out and two empty bean cans and a sausage can lay in the grass, as well as more than a half dozen cigarette butts on a broad flat rock. A pile of human ex-crement decorated the grass just outside the camp area. She could see nothing that mattered to her party, and she signaled the others to come with her to join Ramsey.

When they caught up with the lawyer, he removed his low-crowned hat and brushed back his thick hair. He nodded toward the forested area. "Looks like a herd of horses went through there. Look at the broken twigs and limbs on the trees and brush. Still wet and sappy. Not more than a few hours ago, I'd say. Maddie, try Pirate with the shirt again."

The wolfdog took a quick sniff and headed along the edge of the woods toward a steep rocky incline. He reared up, planted his front feet on the rock and waited for his human friends to catch up to him, then he turned away and went down into a little ravine and started barking. Ramsey clambered down to see what the wolfdog had discovered. He pulled back some brush and tree limbs and hollered. "Saddle and bridle. Somebody unsaddled a horse here and hid the tack."

"Brady," Samantha said. "He would want to save it with the notion of making a dollar if he could find it later."

Darby said, "Well, he probably didn't want to leave a sign he had been here, either."

"Probably not," Samantha agreed, "but he would think about the money first."

Ramsey covered the saddle again, before he came out of the ravine. "We can't take it with us, and it's as protected as it can be right now. It appears he abandoned a horse. But why did the dog lead us to a dead end, and why did the riders break into the woods?"

Darby said, "He must have climbed that rock wall. It looks like it extends north forever."

Samantha said, "The old mine. That's where he was headed. We walked through the trees to find a trail to take us back down to the valley, and we came upon this old mine. Another time, we explored above the mine and found hand and footholds on the wall. Once you get the hang of it, you can move like a monkey on that wall."

"There hasn't been any serious mining around here," Ramsey explained to Darby. "During the California gold rush back in '49, a rumor started that there was gold or silver in these mountains. Would-be miners passing through on the way to California got word and decided to get a jump on the stampede and started panning the streams and mining in the mountains. I understand that is how Lockwood was founded. A man named Frank Lockwood built a general store and tavern to serve the miners and established some freighter roads from Cheyenne and Laramie. Of course, those towns didn't amount to much till the Union Pacific came through over fifteen years later."

Darby asked, "And what about the gold?"

"Nothing. Not an ounce. Fortunately, there is no better farming and ranching country than our valley, and Lockwood is midway between three or four communities in all directions and Cheyenne and Laramie within a few days ride. Frank Lockwood had the foresight to open wagon trails from those areas to his new town, and after the 'little rush,' as it became known, the town survived and eventually thrived."

Darby said, "For whatever reason, it looks like the riders headed through the timber in the direction of the mine. Sammy, how long does it take to get to the mine from here?"

Samantha shrugged, "Ten or fifteen minutes maybe."

"Let's move," Darby said, reining her mount back toward the path that was already broken.

She started to head into the trees when the sound of repeated gunfire to the northwest echoed through the mountains.

# Chapter 26

RUTH WEINTRAUB, A pert, white-clad woman about his age, Trace figured, helped him to a sitting position in his hospital bed and stuffed some pillows behind his back for support. Weintraub's wife and nurse could cure you with her smile, he thought. "Thank you, ma'am. That's fine," he said. She stepped briskly out of the room, leaving him with the room-sharing patient and two visitors sitting in the straight-back chairs at his bedside.

He looked over at the other bed. The man who called himself Roscoe appeared to be sleeping, and Trace knew that the other patient had been treated with a heavy dose of laudanum to help him sleep through the pain. He decided it did not matter whether Roscoe heard the conversation or not.

He turned his head toward Matthew Gaines and Hannah Locke, who had been escorted into the room and seated by the nurse and now looked at him expectantly. "Miss Locke and Matt, thanks for coming by."

"Please, call me Hannah," the young woman said.

"Okay, Hannah, it is."

Gaines said, "I was shocked when Doc told me he had you in a hospital bed over here. He said you wanted to see Hannah, too, so I volunteered to stop by her office."

"Well, I will get right down to business. That fella in the other bed is a part of this, and I need to be making some decisions fast. First I need to bring you up to date." He told the two about the killing of Slick, the man dressed in black, and then the encounter with Roscoe.

"You have been busy since we spoke yesterday," Gaines said. "Makes me feel like I'm getting my money's worth."

"More for you to chew on. I haven't put it all together yet, but some names have come up. Men who may, or may not, have something to do with whatever is going on: Reggie Weaver and Craig Hammer."

Gaines paled and his eyes widened in surprise. "Craig? He works for me." He looked at Hannah. "You two were engaged."

"I am probably the source of Trace's information. I know nothing for sure about Craig's involvement. I just know that county records show he has been making some land purchases that don't make sense, and he would not be above some kind of scheming. That's all. Just keep your eye on him. I wouldn't trust him with any confidential information."

"I certainly won't. I don't confide in him anyway. I have never discussed my hiring of the Pinkerton Agency with him, but he could put something together from my banking transactions that would put him on alert. I should have fired him months ago. I don't think he would embezzle. I have an outside accountant from Cheyenne come in every six months to audit the bank. I have just never felt right about him. Frankly, I wasn't disappointed when you broke off your engagement. You deserve better."

"What about Weaver?" Trace asked.

"I don't know him well, other than by reputation— which isn't good. He doesn't come into the bank much. No accounts. Strictly a cash business. Folks who do business that way generally have something to hide. No, that's not fair. Some just do not trust banks. And banks are just like any other business; some should not be trusted. Anyway, Weaver would certainly bear investigating."

"Well, that's not what I called you over to talk about. I've got a man in the other bed who needs to be locked up. He claims not to know much, but he may know more than he realizes. There also may be some worried folks who aren't sure what he knows. With Brady Yates on the loose, and now Roscoe corralled, they might feel like they are trying to plug a leaky dike. And that tends to bring on panic. That means Roscoe's life isn't worth two cents without our protection." He heard movement in the captive's bed. "You hear that, Roscoe?"

"Yeah," Roscoe said in a screechy voice. "Ain't wanting to die. You keep me safe, and I'll tell you what I know. Ain't much, though."

"That's the question," Trace said. "How do we keep him safe?"

Gaines said, "Why don't you just tell us what you have in mind?"

"I want to move me and Roscoe into the jail this afternoon. Talked to Doc Weintraub. He said okay. He'll come by and check on us when he can. Neither of us is likely to die with the move. Roscoe's more of a mess than I am. The wolfdog about ate him up."

Hannah said, "You're not going to trust Ferd Bullock to protect you and Roscoe?"

"Nope."

"Then what are you going to do with Bullock?"

"Thought I might lock him up."

"But you're not a law officer."

"No. That's why I asked to speak with a law wrangler. Matt's mayor. I want him to appoint me as town marshal. Do you think he has authority to do that?"

"Territorial laws provide for county subdivisions and election of officials but don't provide any law enforcement structure for towns. Our law firm advises the town board, so I am familiar with the town's laws and regulations. The Lockwood town code consists of about ten pages, and I must tell you there is no provision for a town marshal."

"What if Matt went ahead and appointed one anyway?"

"The marshal's authority could be challenged in a court of law, and the appointment would likely be ruled invalid. Of course, somebody would have to file papers with the circuit court to take that action and wait three months for a judge to show up to hear the case. Matt could be removed from office by a recall petition and special election of voters if voters didn't approve."

"Hell," Gaines said, "I get paid five dollars a year for being mayor. I would just resign if folks started fussing about it. But they wouldn't. Who would care but the people who are responsible for the killings? I don't think they'll be showing their faces in the courts. I'm more concerned about what they might do if you've got Ferd locked up, but if you want the job, I hereby appoint you the town marshal. Sorry, I don't have a badge."

"My Pinkerton badge will do. I'll be prepared for company. I don't know how well I can handle a rifle right now, but a bum left shoulder won't interfere with firing my Colt. I'm guessing they have some shotguns in their office armory. I'll keep a loaded shotgun handy. I don't need to have good aim for that."

Gaines said, "I'll go with you when you and your friend here go to the sheriff's office. I can verify your appointment as town marshal. I'll pick up my Smith & Wesson at the bank. I keep weapons in my office in case somebody tries a robbery. Fortunately, they haven't been needed till now."

"Come back about three o'clock," Trace said. "That's when we'll make our move. And when you leave the bank to come over here, tell your vice-president, Mister Hammer, where you are headed and what you are up to."

"Seriously?"

"Seriously. I will be interested to know his reaction."

Gaines said, "But if Craig Hammer is involved, won't that be an invitation for trouble?"

"Just as well get it over with. I'm guessing we'll put together some more pieces to the puzzle while we're at it."

Hannah said, "They won't do anything till after sundown. We need to find you some backup. I'll talk to Jeb Oaks."

"Who is Jeb Oaks?"

Gaines said, "He owns the general store just across the street from the jail. He is a good friend of Ethan's, and he was a buffalo soldier during the Comanche wars. He and his wife, She Bear, and their two kids live on a farmstead just outside of town. I'm sure he would stick around the store late tonight. She Bear works at the store, too, and their little girl and boy play in a back room and behind the store during the day. I can't imagine She Bear missing out on the prospects of a good fight."

Hannah said, "I'll need to run to my house after work and change, but I'll show up at the jail with my Winchester."

"That's not necessary—really."

"This is my town, too."

# Chapter 27

MATT GAINES WALKED into the Weintraub hospital at precisely three o'clock, looking like the usual business-suited banker except for the gun belt and holstered pistol strapped to his waist. His coat did not quite cover the evidence of the weapon beneath it.

When Gaines stepped into the room, Nurse Ruth had just changed bandages on both the patients and was assisting Roscoe into what remained of his buckskin jacket after the wolfdog's shredding. She had washed off the worst of the blood from the garment, but patches of brown stains persisted.

Trace's shoulder was stiff and sore but more an annoyance than painful. He waited for the nurse to slip out of the room. She was a sweetheart, but a determined lady, he thought. Pretty as a picture with that black hair pulled back in a ponytail. She had even shaved him this morning despite his protests that he could handle the task himself. She had admonished him that the shave would be on his bill whether she did it or not, and he had surrendered. He rubbed his hand on the cheeks of his clean-shaven face. Smoother than a barber's shave. He hated letting his whiskers grow for more than a day. He always felt dirty when he missed a daily shave. Well, he had no reason to feel that way now.

Darby had been kind enough to drop off a change of clothes before she headed for the livery this morning, and Nurse Ruth had supervised a bath in a curtained off room with a huge porcelain tub. Under different circumstances, he might have reveled in that experience, but he could not be comfortable with a female pulling back the curtain to check on him at the worst possible moments and then stepping in to clean about the injured shoulder.

Best of all, before kissing him goodbye, Darby had endorsed his purchase of a new jacket to replace the torn and bloodied one, forgetting to suggest a dollar limit. It was almost worth getting shot up for. Not that he would have purchased one anyway. It would just be nice to be able to point out she had not suggested a price when she asked how much it cost. That gorgeous hind end was not the only thing tight about that woman.

Just before she left, Darby had asked him if he had a plan for his day yet. He had replied, "Not yet."

"Liar," she had said. "Please don't do something that gets you shot again." She had walked out without pressing him further.

As he buckled his gun belt, working clumsily with his left hand, Trace looked at Gaines who waited expectantly near the doorway. "Did you tell Hammer?"

"I did. He was sitting at his desk at the time, so I couldn't tell if he pissed his pants. He turned white as a sheet, though, and his hands started shaking like aspen leaves in a stiff wind. I would say he reached panic real fast. He has probably already left the bank for the day."

"Then we had best be walking over to the sheriff's office." Trace turned to Roscoe. "You ready, Roscoe, or whatever your name is?"

"That is my name. Roscoe Smith. I'm telling you true."

"Smith. Not very creative if you are making it up. Let's go." He signaled for the young gunman to take the lead.

When they stepped out onto the boardwalk, Smith asked, "What if somebody's laying for me?"

"I hope they don't hit me by mistake," Trace said.

They crossed the street, and Trace noticed that the black boots he had just wiped down were coated with dust again. With the condition of the prisoner's hands, he would not be able to assign the cleaning task to Mister Smith. Kid probably was not bright enough to do a decent job anyhow.

They reached the sheriff's office without incident. Before they entered, Trace said, "Matt, if you will keep an eye on the prisoner, I will be sure Deputy Bullock is in and see to his arrest."

When he opened the door, the scent of cigarette smoke told him Bullock was in, so he pulled his Army Colt from its holster and stepped in. Bullock sat in the office in his usual foot-on-the-desk position, a smoldering, twisted cigarette hanging from the edge of his lips.

At the sight of Trace's Colt pointed directly at his chest, Bullock swung his legs off the desk and muttered, "What the hell? You're pointing that gun at the law, mister. I could throw you in jail for that."

"Not a smart move, Bullock. Unbuckle your gun belt and drop it on the floor."

"You're crazy. You ain't got no authority to tell me what to do. Get the hell out of here."

"This gun gives me all the authority I need, but I also represent the law. I am now Lockwood's duly appointed town marshal." Trace yelled, "Matt, bring our prisoner in here."

Gaines pushed Smith ahead of him as he stepped inside and closed the door. "Hello, Ferd," Gaines said. "I heard your conversation. As Lockwood's mayor, I appointed Trace Crockett as town marshal." He stepped up beside Trace, pulled his own pistol and leveled it at Bullock. "Do what the marshal says."

Bullock stood up, unbuckled the belt and dropped it with his holstered gun on the floor.

"Go ahead, Trace," Gaines said. "Make it official."

Trace said, "Ferd Bullock. I am placing you under arrest."

"You can't do that," Bullock whined. "What are the charges?"

"We will start with the murder of Sheriff Will Bridges. That's a hanging offense, so any other charges are irrelevant."

Panic in his eyes revealed the truth. The man was at the least a witness. Trace would bet on it. "You can't do that. I didn't even draw my gun," Bullock said.

"But you are admitting you were there?"

"I ain't admitting nothing."

"Matt, if you will keep your gun on this criminal, I am going to search him before we lock him up."

He walked around the desk and instructed Bullock to turn his pockets inside out. The man complied, spilling a key ring with door and cell keys and assorted coins on the floor. He patted down the arrested deputy's torso and ordered Bullock to remove his boots to confirm there were no secreted weapons. Satisfied, Trace took him by the arm and escorted the bewildered man to the nearest of the three cells that lined one side of the open hallway that led to the rear of the narrow room. He wanted the deposed acting sheriff not far from the front desks where they could easily talk and where he could keep an eye on the man.

They placed Roscoe Smith in the back cell in order to put some distance between the two prisoners. The arrangement would prevent any collusion between the two. Trace noted there was no back door to the building. Good to hamper escapes, not so good in the event of a fire.

When Gaines departed, he said, "I will be in the neighborhood before dusk, me and a few of my boys. You won't see us unless it's necessary."

"I appreciate that. Otherwise, we'll talk again in the morning. Now a few practical issues. There are porcelain chamber pots in the cells, so that solves an immediate concern there. I assume there is a privy out back, but I don't want to move these men. How do I feed them?"

"I forgot to tell you. Hannah said she would take care of that. She will send somebody by the office about six o'clock with meals for all of you."

"That was kind of her."

"She can be thoughtful, but she can be riled easy enough, too. Sometimes, you have to tiptoe around her moods, but she's a damn good lawyer, and I'd trust her with my life. There is a word Ethan uses to describe her. What is it? Enigma, that's it. Enigma. Kind of a mystery woman. Don't play poker with her. You'll never figure her out."

After Gaines left, Trace used the keys to open a long steel box on the floor, where he found several rifles and two shotguns, one double-barreled. He removed the shotguns and laid them out on the sheriff's desk. He asked Bullock, who had been watching his every move like a wary hound, "Where are the shells for these?"

"Why in the hell should I tell you?"

"It might save your life."

"You are fixing to kill me? I don't think so."

"I'm not unless you push me to it. But it's time for you to do some thinking if it doesn't make your brain blow up."

"What are you talking about?"

"You've heard us talking. You know we're preparing for an assault on the jail. For what it's worth, Matt told your friend, Craig Hammer, that we were going to arrest you and jail Roscoe. If you had been out and about like a good sheriff should be, you would have learned that I brought in a man named Slick last night. Dressed in black. His corpse is at the undertakers. Now, think. If we have visitors come tonight, do you really think they would be coming to break you out of jail? What use are you to them now? You are a liability. They need to shut you up. Roscoe, too. Anybody that comes will be coming to kill you."

He raised his voice so Smith could hear. "Did you hear what I said, Mister Smith? I suggest you both be thinking about telling me what you know."

Bullock said, "There's a box of shells in the lower, left-side drawer, shoved to the back."

# Chapter 28

TROUBLE GRABBED TAG'S mane and rope reins, leaped, and scrambled onto the gelding's back. He nudged the horse downslope on the trail that led away from the mine, moving slowly because the rapidly melting snow made footing a bit slippery in spots and he harbored some uncertainty about controlling the horse without a bit and bridle. As they rode on, he was pleased to find that the sorrel was responsive to gentle tugs of reins along its neck.

He heard voices behind him up the trail, loud and angry. The pursuers had obviously broken out of the woods and found the mine and would be looking to confirm he had been present there. They would not tarry long. There would be ample evidence in the patches of remaining snow that he had been there, that he was mounted and precisely where he had made his exit.

Several gunshots resolved any doubt. He tossed a look over his shoulder. Three riders, perhaps a hundred yards back. He kneed his gelding, and the horse lurched forward, moving down the slope at surprising speed. The crack of more gunshots. He could not outrun a bullet, and sooner or later one of the riders would start to close the gap. He was like a rabbit giving a dog a good run against bad odds. Another shot, and he felt a burning pain in his ribs. For an instant, he wondered if that was all he would feel before he died, but sure-footed Tag kept moving, forcing him to focus on controlling the horse.

Trouble saw that they were approaching a sharp bend in the trail. As he neared the turn, he realized that the old road at this juncture edged one of the countless narrow canyons that sliced between towering mountainsides. Going straight ahead, the trail would have dropped any traveler into the abyss. The walls were rough and craggy, steep but not sheer. He reined in the sorrel, grabbed his rifle, and slid off. He slapped the horse sharply on the rump, hoping it would move on and not want to hang around.

The horse did not budge, and he slapped the gelding again with more force before it started moving on at a walk. Some speed would have been welcome, but at least his mount might lead gunmen down the trail for a spell and give him a chance to hide.

He slipped over the canyon rim, sliding some fifteen feet to a narrow ledge, where he planted his feet. He did not think he would be seen here if the hunters kept their mounts to the inside of the trail, which would be the instinct of most riders. And until they caught up with Tag, the men would not likely consider that the rabbit would have escaped over the canyon rim.

Trouble clutched his rifle and pressed his back to the canyon wall when he heard the clickety-clack of shoed horses on the stone trail above. He heard voices, but could not make out any words as they rode past. He let out a sigh of relief and turned around to face the canyon expanse. He guessed that the floor, barely wide enough to allow passage of the stream that threaded through it, was several hundred feet below. If he could make his way down the side, the stream would eventually lead him to the valley or another trail.

He felt the wetness from blood soaking his shirt and coat along his left side and was concerned about the weakness that was threatening to buckle his legs, but he did not have time to tend to it till he found a place to hide. He took several steps along the ledge, seeking a route to a lower level. Suddenly, he felt the rock beneath him crumbling away. He started to step to solid footing before he realized the entire ledge was disappearing and he was catapulted into the air, releasing his rifle as if he momentarily had the illusion he could fly. He hit a shale slope below him, slid with the stones as they dropped over a ledge and slammed him onto a stone outcropping. He heard the snap before he felt the pain in his lower right leg.

Trouble blacked out briefly following the impact. When he awakened, he knew that he would not be descending to the bottom of the canyon. His leg was broken, and the pain was all-consuming. His ribs were competing with the broken bone for torment now, too, and he did not have the strength to examine either. He just wanted to sleep. He did not much care if death awaited in the darkness so long as it carried the hurt away. He closed his eyes in surrender.

# Chapter 29

THE GUNFIRE HAD stopped by the time Darby and her party broke into the clearing near the old mine. Ramsey was already on the ground roaming the area like a birddog scaring up game. The real dog, Pirate, was barking at the entrance of the mine shaft, removing any doubt that Brady Yates had been in the cave.

Maddie and Samantha were with the dog. Maddie called, "He stayed here. There are some food crumbs on the floor . . . or were. Pirate cleaned them up."

Darby stayed with the horses, allowing the others to investigate the site. She thought about the gunfire. The shots had sounded further away than the distance to this place. It had taken no more than fifteen minutes for the party to arrive here even with the obstacles presented by the tangle of brush and timber. No, if Brady Yates had been here, he departed before the guns were fired. She could see the hoofprints now in the fragments of melting snow angling downslope toward what might have been a wagon trail at one time.

Ramsey strolled over to her. "One horse with a chipped shoe that matches the track of the one that went close to the wall not far from where the saddle and tack were hidden. My guess is that Brady is riding bareback, but it makes no sense. Why in blazes would he dump the saddle if he kept the horse?"

"Darby, Mister Ramsey, come here a minute. I think you should look at this. If you've got a candle and a lucifer, bring them."

Darby sighed. They needed to be moving on. The gunfire had been an ominous sign, and they should get to the source. Yet, Maddie generally had solid instincts about the importance of her observations. "I have a candle in my saddlebags," she hollered back. She and Ramsey tied the mounts to pine branches along the site's fringe and walked up to the mine opening where they met Maddie, who was holding out a small black object in her hand.

Maddie said, "I thought you said this was a gold mine."

"Attempted gold mine," Ramsey said, "But you are holding the black kind."

"Coal?" Darby asked, plucking the object from Maddie's hand. "Were they mining coal here?"

"Never been any coal mining here, but it's getting to be a big business northeast of here where the railroad has connected."

"I think there are fresh diggings here," Maddie said. "Light the candle. I will show you." Evidently sensing Darby's anxiety about moving on, she added. "It will only take a minute."

Darby gave Ramsey the coal chunk, struck a lucifer on the wall, lit the candle and handed it to Maddie, who motioned the others to follow her into the shaft. The tunnel extended only a short distance, but Darby saw where the shaft had been extended perhaps ten feet beyond its previous dead-end. Coal lumps were scattered about the floor and she could make out what appeared to be black veins of rock on the walls. She could not say for certain what she was seeing, for she knew next to nothing about mineral mining of any kind.

"You're right," Ramsey said, "somebody's been digging here recently, but there hasn't been much coal removed."

"We have got to stay on Trouble's trail," Darby admonished.

Ramsey said, "Let's move out."

After they saddled up and headed toward the old wagon trail, Darby said, "We will need to be silent and keep eyes and ears wide open." She nodded for Ramsey to take the lead again and he reined the Appaloosa to the front as the others moved into single file behind him.

Less than a half hour later, Darby heard men yelling to each other from around a bend in the wagon trail. Ramsey signaled a halt and waved for Darby to come up beside him.

"I think they are moving this way," Ramsey said.

Darby said, "Why don't we just get the horses into the trees and wait for them. If they've got Brady, our best chance to take him would be to surprise this bunch."

"I agree," Ramsey said, dismounting and pulling a Winchester from its scabbard and leading his Appaloosa off the trail.

The others followed his lead. Even Samantha had a rifle ready. "I've never shot at a person," Samantha whispered to Darby as they tied their horses to tree branches and moved to the brush along the trail's edge.

Ramsey dashed to the other side, after admonishing everyone to place their shots away from his location. "I'll do the same. We don't want to shoot each other."

"Sammy," Darby said, responding to the girl's concern. "I don't think this is a good time to shoot somebody, and I hope you never do. The gun is for your protection. Use it only if you are forced in order to protect yourself." She pressed a finger to her lips. "Listen."

Three riders came around the bend in the trail, one leading a haltered sorrel. That would be Brady's. An ominous sign, she feared. Gunslinger types, one heavyset with a black beard split by a broad white strip like he was carrying a skunk on his chin. The other two were younger, lean and rawboned and would pass for ordinary cowhands were it not for the guns slung low on their hips. One was noticeably taller, and lightly bronzed skin suggested some Indian or Mexican ancestry. The other was fair-skinned and ruddy-faced with scraggly, blond chin whiskers and a droopy moustache that needed trimming.

Darby was surprised, as they approached, that the riders had not spotted the waiting ambushers, but they seemed engaged in earnest conversation. As they neared, Skunk spoke to the others, his voice raspy and loud. "I say we gotta go back down. We're past the place we last seen the kid. You sure you hit the little bastard, Vince?"

The blond man answered, "I ain't blind. I seen him start to slip from the horse's back after I fired, and then he straightened up and disappeared around the bend. And you saw the blood on the horse's flank."

Skunk said, "Well, shit, let's turn around and go back where we found the horse, but I couldn't pick up no sign. And you two ain't worth a horse turd when it comes to tracking." He swung his horse around when his eyes suddenly fixed on the surrounding forest.

He had sighted her, Darby knew. She yelled, "Drop your guns. You are surrounded."

Skunk drew his revolver from its holster and aimed it, but Darby squeezed her Winchester's trigger and dropped him from the saddle. The other two gunslingers started firing wildly, their horses rearing and circling in fear. Ramsey was firing his rifle from the other side, and Maddie was levering cartridges and squeezing off shots even after all the riders lay on the ground.

It had happened so quickly. One second a man was drawing his pistol, and less than a minute later, three men lay on the ground. Darby stepped out of the woods and walked cautiously to the bloody forms strewn on the trail. The others joined her, and Ramsey was stooping next to the bodies, giving a negative shake of his head as he checked each one.

Ramsey stood and announced, "All dead. The older fellow took one dead center in the chest. At this short range, that was all it took. The other two are pretty much shot up. Never get used to it. One minute a man's breathing and fighting. Next one, he's gone. Life on this earth is over. I don't care what kind of man takes your bullet, it's never a good feeling to kill a man. Not for me anyway."

Darby silently agreed. "We'll need to do something with the bodies. I guess the horses will come with us. But the question is, what became of Brady?"

Samantha said, "It sounded like he was wounded." She took a few steps down the trail and hollered, "Brady, it's Sammy. You are safe now. I am with friends. Come out or yell so we can find you."

Everyone waited for a response. Silence. Samantha called again. No answer.

They started gathering up the newly acquired horses to secure until they figured out what to do next. The sorrel reared back when Darby reached for the rope halter, turned away and started trotting down the trail in the direction from which the gunfighters had come. Pirate followed the horse.

"Pirate," Maddie called, "come back here."

The wolfdog ignored her, so she started racing after him. Darby lost sight of all three when the group rounded the turn in the trail. "I suppose I'd better go after them," Darby told Ramsey just before Pirate's frenzied barking erupted.

"Maybe we should all go," Ramsey said.

Darby and Ramsey retrieved their horses, but Samantha raced ahead. When they walked around the bend leading their mounts, the girl was already with the others. The wolfdog was on the edge of the canyon rim still barking frantically, and Maddie's fingers were gripped on the sorrel's halter steadying the mount.

Maddie said, "Brady's down there someplace, but I don't see anything. There is dried blood on the horse's back, so he must have been riding it. I would bet they separated here. If he didn't fall off, he dismounted."

"Maybe he thought he could hide under the rim's overhang," Ramsey said.

Samantha said, "I think he would head for the bottom of the canyon and try to follow the stream back to Lockwood. He was always saying 'Follow the water. Sooner or later, it gets you to people, and you won't die of thirst.'"

"Wise young man," Ramsey commented. "Look." He pointed to wet dirt where shale and rocks had been recently disturbed. "You're right, Sammy. He was moving toward the canyon floor. He was on his feet for a spell and then started sliding, and there is nasty drop-off down there. I don't like it. And from here, we can't see below the edge of the drop."

Darby said, "There is an outcropping of rock that extends from the canyon wall below the drop-off. The slide angles that direction, but I don't see any sign of him. If he kept going, I don't have much hope."

Samantha said, "He's alive. I know he is. We just have to find him"

Darby understood. The attachment between Sammy and Brady seemed to be something most folks searched a lifetime for and never found. And it was not about romantic love. It was a connection beyond that. Romance was just a bonus for those who found it. She wasn't certain Sammy would accept Brady's death if she stood over his cold, dead body. She counted herself one of those lucky ones. She and Trace shared such a bond, she felt, along with the bonus.

"Pirate, wait," Maddie scolded as the wolfdog disappeared over the canyon rim. "Come back. Damn him. He only obeys when it suits him."

Like his mistress, Darby thought.

# Chapter 30

PIRATE MADE HIS journey down the steep wall appear easy. He was a huge animal, his weight pushing 150 pounds on a tall, long frame. Darby knew the wolfdog outweighed any of the females present by a good amount. Yet, he negotiated the rocks seemingly without disturbing the smallest stone or sliver of shale. He moved laterally back and forth, apparently sniffing up old goat or other animal paths as he worked his way down.

Pirate disappeared for a time when he headed to a spot where the drop-off tapered and merged into the ledge that connected with the outcropping. Suddenly, his mournful howling sent a shiver racing down Darby's spine.

"My God," Maddie said. "He's found Brady."

Samantha went to the lip of the canyon's rim and began calling for Brady again, but the only response was the wolfdog's howling. "I've got to get down there," Samantha said.

"No," Darby said. "You will stay put." She turned to Ramsey. "I am going to do this. Two of the hired guns' horses had coiled ropes attached to the saddles. I'm sure they weren't for roping cattle, but we can use them now."

"Why don't you let me do this?" Ramsey said.

"You're needed more up here. You're stronger than any of us, and I'm betting you have had experience on the saddle end of the rope if we need to use one of the horse's as an anchor. I wouldn't know how to go about that."

"I suppose you're right. My gelding has helped with hoisting a load several times. We can hitch one end to his saddle horn or shoulders for backup if we need it." Ramsey handed the Appaloosa's reins to Samantha. "Sammy, would you hold Patch here while Darby and I fetch some ropes?"

"And, Maddie," Darby said, "maybe you could convince Pirate we are on our way, and that he can quiet down a bit."

"I'll try, but he's got his own mind about such things."

Darby, leading her mare, walked back up the trail with Ramsey, who led the sorrel that they assumed had paired up with Brady. "Ethan, I'm not optimistic about what I'm going to find down there."

"I understand, but Brady Yates is a tough kid. And if it is Brady, in whatever condition, we've got to bring him out."

They collected two lariats and found some braided rawhide rope in Brady's possible bag. Darby assumed it had furnished the reins and halter for the sorrel. Darby found a small hatchet with the gear strapped to one of the dead men's horses and placed it in the growing pile of guns and knives they had been collecting from Brady's pursuers.

On their way back, Darby said, "We still need to keep an eye out. There could be others out there looking for Brady. If some heard the gunfire, they could be coming this way."

"I've been watching. It's easy enough to see riders coming from downslope. I'm more concerned about somebody coming from the direction of the mine. It's not too likely, though. Most would probably figure the gunshots were directed at Brady and that they had lost their chance to earn whatever bonus was offered for his hide."

The wolfdog had quieted some when they reached the others, offering only an occasional bark, evidently to remind the humans that he was waiting. Samantha still called for Brady intermittently, and Darby could see the girl was on the brink of hysteria.

"Sammy, I'm going down there. I will let you know immediately what I find. You know, of course, Brady may not even be there."

"He's there," she said.

Ramsey was tying the ropes together, and she turned to him, "I hope you know your knots."

He smiled, "A square knot to bind ropes of the same size, a sheet bend to join a lariat with the narrower rawhide rope, and a bowline for the loop on the passenger end. It won't slip to squeeze you."

"I am impressed."

"I worked with an old Army sergeant who was a sailor from Boston before he joined the horse soldiers."

"Boston. My hometown."

"Irish?"

"Yes. Trace teases me about my Irish lilt. I am unaware of it, of course."

"Your lilt is charming. Hang on to it."

"I wouldn't know how to lose it."

"I think we're about ready. I am going to hitch our end of the rope to Patch. He's just backup. I'll lower you down the wall and call on the young ladies for help if I need it."

Darby asked, "Do we have enough rope?"

"I stepped off well over a hundred feet. It's hard to judge the distance from here, but we should be close. If you can't reach the outcropping, you should at least be able to look below the overhang and see what the wolfdog is howling about."

"Okay, let's go." Darby picked up the end of the rope and slipped the loop over her head and shoulders and positioned it around her chest and under her arms, grateful for small breasts on this mission.

Ramsey finished anchoring the other rope end to the Appaloosa's saddle horn, then started coiling it into loops to take up slack. When he neared Darby, he said, "Okay, take it slow. I've got you." He turned to Maddie, "Why don't you stand beside me, Maddie? Be ready to grab the rope if I ask for help."

Darby dropped over the rim and almost lost her footing when she landed on the shale incline, but she held tight to the taut rope till she regained her balance, noting that, as Ramsey had promised, the loop held firm and did not tighten around her chest. She inched her way down the steep canyon wall as Ramsey slowly let the rope follow her. She slipped several more times, but the rope held fast, and she quickly righted herself. As she neared the edge of the drop-off, she tensed and stopped.

Clutching the rope, she leaned out and looked over the edge and for the first time saw Brady "Trouble" Yates, his form crumpled up against the rock wall just under the overhang. The pale boy's eyes were shut, and his shirt and jacket blood soaked. His right leg was twisted at an unnatural angle. She was at least ten feet above the ledge and could not detect any breathing. His body was still as a corpse. Oh, God, he cannot be dead. He cannot be. The big wolfdog sat beside the boy looking up expectantly at Darby with those haunting yellow eyes.

She stepped back and looked up to the rim where Ramsey clutched the rope with Maddie holding tightly behind him. She yelled, "Brady's down here. He's hurt, but I can't tell how badly. I need to get to the ledge, but I won't have any footing."

Ramsey hollered back, "We can hold you, but we have only about fifteen feet of rope to give you. Is that enough?"

"I think so. I'm going now." She turned and sat down, scooting to the edge of the drop-off with her legs dangling over the rim. She grasped the rope and slid off the jagged precipice. She dropped several feet before jolting to a halt that felt like her shoulder bones were being ripped from their sockets. She was suspended like a ragdoll in the air above ledge. She looked up and saw that the rope was stuck in a crevice in the overhang, her own weight wedging it there.

"Darby, are you on the ledge?" Ramsey's voice.

"No, Ethan. The rope is stuck in a crack in the rock."

She looked down. A five-foot drop for her feet that would land her a few feet from the boy. No option. She lifted her arms above her head, slipped through the loop and hit the ledge, falling backward and landing on her buttocks partway onto the escarpment that extended outward from the ledge. The impact sent a stabbing shock up her spine that numbed her legs for a few moments before the wolfdog started barking and reminded her of her purpose.

"Darby?"

"I'm all right, Ethan. I dropped to the ledge."

"Thank God. The rope's loose, and you weren't on it. I was afraid . . ."

"I'm fine. I'm going to check Brady."

She stiffly raised herself to her knees and crawled over to the boy, getting a shot of renewed strength when she saw the rise and fall of his chest. "He's alive," she yelled. "He's alive."

She knelt next to Brady and unbuttoned the bloody shirt and coat, peeling back the garments and searching for the wound. The search was brief. The blood flow had ebbed to occasional drips from the right side of the rib cage. The area was caked with drying blood, but she could feel a furrow beneath the skin that sheathed the ribs. She could not find an exit wound and thought it likely that the slug was still lodged somewhere, hopefully at a location where it was not doing more damage.

She touched his cheek. "Brady," she said. "I am a friend. Can you hear me?"

Brady's eyes opened and closed, and his head turned ever so slightly toward her, a signal that there was life there. She turned her attention to his leg and traced her fingers down his injured limb. She thought she felt a swollen mass three or four inches below his knee, but his denim trousers blocked examination. She was scolding herself for not carrying a knife when she saw the sheathed knife on Brady's belt. She reached over and removed it, discovering a skinning knife, a tool every bit as sharp as Trace kept his.

Darby easily split the trouser leg and tugged the fabric apart to reveal a scrawny leg, badly swollen and red where she had detected the injury. She was certain there was a break and some bone separation, but there was nothing protruding through the flesh. But how would they get him out of this place?

She stood and yelled at Ramsey, trying to explain what she had found.

He was silent for several moments. Finally, he called, "I'm coming down."

# Chapter 31

"DARBY." IT WAS Ramsey's voice. "I'm just above, but I can't see you."

She moved out from under the overhang to the stone outcropping and saw him, resting on his hip, one hand clutched to the rope. "You made it. I thought you were crazy. How can Maddie and Sammy pull anybody out of here."

"I made a harness over Patch's shoulder and chest, and Maddie's holding his reins. Sammy will keep an eye on us and relay instructions. Those gals are 'weasel smart' as a friend of mine always says. Now, we have got work to do. We don't have more than an hour of sunlight left, and we don't want to be going up this wall in the dark."

Darby said, "Just tell me what you've got in mind."

"I will have to stay where I'm at to keep the rope from binding when you bring Brady out. I'm afraid you are going to have to stabilize his leg on your own. You do have a knife?"

"Yes, Brady's."

"What's he wearing on his feet?"

"I call them work shoes. Trace would say they are clod-hoppers."

"And I am wearing moccasins. They won't help."

"I don't understand."

"I can't think of anything else we could use as a temporary splint. Boot shafts."

Darby said, "My boots."

"That's all we've got."

"Tell me what to do."

Ramsey said, "You will need some cloth strips to anchor the splint."

Darby said, "I'm wearing a wool shirt under my pullover doeskin. I'll sacrifice it. I have a spare shirt rolled up in my bedroll, anyway."

"Good enough. First task: cut off the boot shafts down to the tongue. Try not to split the shafts. We want to end up with two tubes."

"I think I see what we're going to do."

Darby sat down and removed her boots and commenced carving with Brady's skinning knife. When the boot shafts were pulled free, she slipped her feet into what remained of her footwear, the topless boots feeling loose and strange. "I've got the shafts cut off," she called to Ramsey. "Just a few minutes and I will be ready."

She pulled off her sheepskin jacket and set it aside, struck by the sudden cold that came with the biting wind. The sunshine had been deceiving her. Quickly, she wriggled out of the doeskin pullover and slipped out of the wool shirt, leaving her only with her camisole. She redressed without the shirt and began reducing the garment to cloth strips.

"I am going to bind his ribs first," she said. "The bleeding will start again when we try to move him." She worked her fingers under Brady's coat and began dressing the wound with crude wraps. The boy shifted and moaned, obviously feeling some pain.

"Did you hear that?" Darby said.

"I'll take that as a positive sign," Ramsey replied.

"I've got the wound wrapped. I'm ready to try the leg."

"Tell me about the leg."

"The swelling is below the knee at least four inches, but the knee bends at a strange angle. As I said before, the bone isn't protruding, but I'm afraid of what happens when we try to move him."

"That's what we're going to deal with. Can you straighten the leg?"

Ron Schwab

"I'll try." She grasped her hand around the twisted leg and slowly moved it, pleased to find little resistance.

"No, no. Don't," Brady mumbled. "Please." She glanced at the boy's face and saw that his eyes were squeezed tight, releasing a few tears at the corners.

"It's straightened pretty well," she said, "but the swelling looks worse."

"Now push the boot shafts over the leg. We want to cover the knee to keep it from bending but be sure there is enough of one of the shafts to cover the break," Ramsey said.

"The shafts are slipping on these skinny legs without any problem," Darby reported. "They won't be as snug as we might like."

"You still have cloth strips, I hope. Tie as many as possible around the shafts as tight as you can. Leave enough cloth to tie his legs together after that. Below the knee and at the ankles. If you don't have enough, I can donate my shirt."

"I should have just enough. But why?"

"To help keep the damaged leg stable when we're pulling him up this slope."

That made sense, but she doubted she would have ever thought of it. When Darby was finished, she said,

"I've done all I can do. The sun's going to be setting soon. How do we get out of here?"

Ramsey dropped the loop end of the rope to the ledge. "This will be the toughest part. Once we get the two of you this far, I can help the rest of the way, it will be easy enough after that."

Darby knew the man was lying, but his intentions were good. "What do you want me to do?"

"Can you lift him?"

Darby studied the sleeping form draped over the cold stones.

"He's not very big, but he is a thirteen-year-old boy and well-muscled. He probably weighs as much, or a bit more than I do."

"Look at the rope loop. I've changed the knot."

"And I suppose you have a name for it." It seemed Ramsey could not resist the opportunity to teach, and she would give him his teaching moment.

"As a matter of fact, it is called a taut line hitch. It can be tightened around an object but once pressure is applied it won't give or squeeze any tighter."

"And the object will be Darby Crockett and Brady Yates?"

"You've got it. Now you get down next to Brady and put that loop around yourself just like before. Then you maneuver the boy up in your lap, slip the loop under his arms, too. Slide the knot, so the loop tightens around the two of you. Make it snug. It won't get any tighter than you make it. Then you will wrap your arms about his chest and hold him tight. Forget about the wound and leg for now. All that counts is getting the two of you out."

Darby said, "I don't know when I've been this scared."

"It will work. I promise. You just close your eyes and hang on to Brady. You may scratch and bruise your back some going over, and you will have sore shoulders, but that's the worst of it."

It was easy to make a promise when the promisee would not be alive to hold you to account, Darby thought. She moved in close to the boy and started work on creating what she thought of as a human pendulum. When she had the rope snugged and a writhing Brady captured in her arms, she said, "I guess I'm ready, but he's squirming. I hope to hell I can hold him."

"Hold tight."

She felt the jolt of the rope under her arms when the rope started lifting her to her feet. She squeezed her eyes shut and clutched Brady when her feet rose off the ledge, and they were suspended in the air. They were in flight, but she did not feel like a soaring eagle. Her thigh and her buttocks slammed against sharp stones several times, and then her back settled on what now seemed like a pillow of cactus. She opened her eyes and saw Ramsey bent over her and the wolfdog watching from off to the side. She was glad he had found his own way out.

"Are you okay?"

"I guess. I'm alive."

"I don't want to move the boy. We'll keep going up the slope. I'll be right beside you."

"I am going to be Brady's sled, so to speak."

"So to speak."

"My butt will be raw meat when this is done."

# Chapter 32

TRACE LOADED BOTH shotguns and laid them out on the sheriff's desk. Then he set the deadbolt lock on the door. He felt suddenly exhausted and dropped down in the chair behind the desk, swinging his feet onto the desktop. He pulled his hat down on his forehead and closed his eyes, nodding off to sleep.

He nearly fell out of his chair when he was awakened by sharp rapping on the door. He rolled the chair back and got to his feet, his hand instinctively reaching for his Colt. "Who is it?"

"Hannah Locke and She Bear. We've brought supper for you and the prisoners."

He went to the door and unbolted it and saw Hannah Locke attired now in boots and britches with hair tied back in a ponytail. She carried a covered plate in each hand. Beside her stood a tall Indian woman, exotically beautiful with dark, searching eyes that said she was sizing him up. She also held two plates.

"This is my friend, She Bear, Jeb's wife, from the general store across the street. She volunteered to help me pick up meals from the restaurant."

He stepped away from the door and waved the women in. "Uh, pleased to meet you, She Bear." He wondered if she spoke English. Her fringed doeskins and braided hair gave her the look of a woman fresh from a Sioux village.

She Bear said, "My pleasure, Mister Crockett. We are delighted to have the Pinkertons in town to help us out. Will Bridges was more than our sheriff. He was a good friend to most of us. We want his killer brought to justice, and I am concerned about Trouble Yates. He is a special young man."

So much for She Bear's language problems. "Well, I appreciate your bringing the meals. Thank you."

The women set the plates down on the deputy's desk. Hannah said, "Thanks, She Bear. I'm sure I will see you later."

She Bear whisked out of the office so quietly, Trace wondered if she had been an illusion. He noticed Hannah had moved to the sink along the southside wall and was filling a coffee pot from the handpump there.

"Can I help?" Trace asked.

"You can toss a few more logs in the woodstove. It's burned down to a few coals."

"I'm embarrassed to say I fell asleep. I could use the coffee. Sorry to be so much trouble."

"You have good reason to be tired. You should probably still be in a bed at Doc Weintraub's. And it is no trouble. Note that I have four plates. I am dining with you this evening, and then I will take up one of the shotguns and stick around. If we are forced to be up all night, we can take shifts."

He opened the stove door and stirred the coals with a poker before feeding a few chunks of wood through the opening. "You can handle a shotgun?"

"Or one of the Winchesters, if you prefer."

Trace straightened up and shrugged. "A shotgun would be good. You seem to know your way around here."

"I often had lunch over here with Will. I made better coffee than his, which isn't saying much. You might say he was a father figure of sorts to me." She turned to Trace. "If you will open the cell doors and cover me, I can give the prisoners their plates and utensils. They will have to wait for coffee."

After feeding the prisoners, Trace ate at the sheriff's desk, and Hannah dined at the deputy's desk. Trace, upon smelling the steak, fried potatoes, and beans under the dish's cover, found he suddenly had an appetite. There was also a serving of apple cobbler on one side of the large plate.

There was an uncomfortable silence between them until Trace spoke. "The meal tastes as good as it looks. Thanks again for taking care of this. I probably wouldn't have thought about feeding the prisoners until I got hungry myself."

Hannah looked up and smiled. "I'm glad you are enjoying it. The menu wasn't gourmet, perhaps, but I've never heard an objection to a good steak out here in the territory."

"Speaking of the territory, Darby and I didn't have a chance to talk much before she left, but she did say you are Myles Locke's daughter. I know Myles. He is our personal lawyer in Manhattan, and we worked with him on a mutual case. He is a very respected man. The case is how we ended up in the Kansas Flint Hills. You're a long way from home."

"My mother died when my twin brother and I were born. My father turned us over to my mother's sister and her husband to raise on their Flint Hills ranch. They provided us a wonderful home, but my father was only an occasional part of my life. After I finished high school, I had some money saved back for me from my mother's small estate, and I took a train to Denver. Several law firms in that city accepted women for clerking positions and I was fortunate enough to find one. I worked there over two years before heading north to Cheyenne."

Trace said, "A big move, going from civilized Denver to untamed Wyoming Territory."

Hannah said, "What first attracted my attention was that women had been granted the vote in the early days of the territory's beginning. Some have suggested that the males' generosity arose from a desire to lure wives to the lonely land. The motives didn't matter to me. I just liked the idea of political equality. But I have since discovered that all that counts out here is doing your job, and the roles of men and women are less structured in the territory. Mothers and wives in the home are valued, but there are few women whose responsibilities stop at the kitchen."

"That's true over most of the west," Trace observed.

Hannah continued, "Most can ride a horse and rope a calf when called upon. Men and women are partners in survival. She Bear is in the general store with Jeb when she's not taking care of the home and kids. She has her own herd of a dozen milk cows that she and a neighbor wife milk twice a day. The neighbor churns butter, and they sell milk and butter in town. She Bear told me they hope to double the herd eventually, maybe make and sell cheese."

"And you didn't stay in Cheyenne," Trace said.

"No. I clerked and read the law with a Cheyenne lawyer, but he had already taken on an associate before I came there and had told me he wouldn't be in a position to employ another lawyer when I was admitted to the bar. I would have been welcome to stay on, but at a clerk's wages."

"That would have been a waste of your education."

"But he told me about a highly regarded lawyer in Lockwood who was looking for an associate and could not find anyone who was willing to live that far from a major city. A lot of people don't thrive in an isolated community. I knew I would, and I took a stagecoach here, walked into Ethan Ramsey's office and left with a job an hour later. After two years, he made me a full partner. I don't say that because I was a special find or anything. I think he was desperate not to be looking for help again. I didn't tell him there was no way I was leaving unless he booted me down the road."

"Not likely, I'll bet."

"This is where I want to make my life. The mountains, the people. It's like this place was just waiting for me to find it. I really sound silly, don't I?"

"Not at all. We're lucky if we can find such a place during our lifetimes. Oddly, I found mine in the Kansas Flint Hills, where you were born and raised."

"Where are your roots?"

"Tennessee. Family had a horse and cow ranch there. War ended that. While my dad was off to war, the Yankees came. Killed most of the livestock. Murdered my grandfather and my mother—after they were done with her. When Dad came home, we moved to Arkansas and he took a bank job in Fort Smith. He was a smart man. No, he was a wise man. There is a difference."

"He's not living?"

"No. Killed in a bank robbery. I still worship him. Miss him every day. Jimmy, my brother, works in the same bank now."

"I hardly know my father. I saw him for Sunday dinners. When I attended high school in Manhattan, my brother and I stayed weekdays and nights at his home in town, but we were in school during the day. Of course, he worked many nights, and when he was there, conversations were very awkward between us."

Trace teased, "You don't work nights?"

"It's different. I don't have children. I must say my twin brother, Thad, doesn't share my resentment. He and my father seem to have a good relationship."

"I've met Thad. He's the veterinarian."

"Yes. He's also a licensed medical doctor."

"So I have heard. You also have two lawyer brothers and a preacher in the family. I've met Cam, but your father said the other brothers live in Nebraska."

"The others are considerably older. They are half-brothers from my father's first wife. They were almost on their own when my mother died. They remained with my father, of course."

Trace liked Hannah, but he found himself uncomfortable with the conversation. He had not come to Wyoming to deal with the woman's simmering anger at her father. He abruptly changed the subject. "Sun's going down. We'd better pay attention to what's going on outside."

# Chapter 33

TRACE GOT OUT of his chair and stepped to one of the narrow, barred windows set on each side of the door. He looked out onto the street. Quiet. No sign of activity except for a lone rider slumped in his saddle riding slowly down the middle of the dusty street in their direction. Suddenly, an explosion roared from down the street, the resulting tremors breaking the window glass and launching shards into his face. He stumbled back, eyes searching for Hannah, who was on her feet now, a double-barreled shotgun readied in her hands.

"What was that?" Hannah asked.

"Dynamite. South, down the street a few buildings. I'd like to check it out, but we'd better stay put."

"I wonder if it's the bank? Maybe somebody's robbing the bank."

"Not likely," Trace said. "Too much of a coincidence. It's a diversion from whatever they're planning for us."

Then he thought of the rider he had seen on the street. He returned to the window just in time to see the man release a flaming bottle that was arcing toward the jail's roof. He heard the explosion on the rooftop as he drew his Colt to fire, he got off a quick shot but did not know if he hit the target, because two more shots came from the general store before the rider toppled from his saddle and the horse raced away in panic.

"Hannah, they are trying to burn us out," Trace warned. He peered out the window and saw that more riders were coming now, closing in from the north and south, perhaps as many as a dozen all told.

Hannah yelled, "Trace, I can smell the smoke. The roof's afire."

"Break the other window with your gun butt and take a position there. If anybody comes toward the door, blast away. I've got to release the prisoners in case we have to get out of here fast."

He snatched up the keys from the desk and rushed down the row of three jail cells to the back of the building where Roscoe Smith was incarcerated. He unlocked the cell. Smith sat on the edge of one of the cell's two cots, and the occupant looked up at Trace with fearful eyes.

"Get up, Smith. Head up front, sit down in one of the wall chairs till I tell you what to do. Don't try to make a break for it. You are as likely to be gunned down by your own people as by one of us. Understand?"

Smith stumbled to his feet. "Yessir. I know that. I ain't doing nothing but what you say."

"Smart man. You might find your way out of this mess yet."

Trace moved back up the hallway to the other cell and unlocked the door for Bullock. He could hear gunfire in the street outside the building, and he turned when he heard the roar of the shotgun. Hannah was at the window ready to unloose the other barrel.

"We're getting help from Jeb and She Bear," she hollered. "I think Matt and some of his hands are down by the bank, but it looks like they're dealing with a fire there. Somebody's on the rooftop of the cobbler's shop with a rifle, and he's on our side. He's downed at least two, maybe more."

"I'll be with you in a minute." He looked up and saw that flames were beginning to eat their way through the ceiling.

"Let me the hell out of here," Bullock demanded.

"Did you hear what I told Smith?" Trace asked. "Same goes for you."

"I heard. I ain't stupid. I ain't going nowhere without you."

Trace thought he could win a debate on the question of Bullock's stupidity, but he pulled the cell door open and said, "Out."

Bullock did not have to be told twice. He darted out of the cell and went directly to the other wall chair next to Smith. He sat down, his wide and fearful eyes watching the flames climbing down the outer wall of the cell from which he had just been freed.

Trace joined Hannah at the window. "We've got about ten minutes before the smoke chases us out of here. What's happening outside?"

"I can't see much. Between the smoke coming off this building and the smoke drifting up the street from the fire down that way, Main Street is like a dense fog."

"Well, we're going to be forced to vacate. I hope we don't get shot by some of our own people. Get another shell in your scattergun and get ready to follow me out. The prisoners will follow us."

"We ought to push them ahead of us," Hannah said.

"Yeah, but they're like the gold in our safe. We need to keep them alive."

"I know. I couldn't do that anyway."

"You're soft. Of course, I couldn't either, not unless I put guns in their hands first."

They were all coughing and choking when they lined up at the door, but there was only a smattering of gunfire now. Trace slid back the deadbolt and swung back the door to be greeted by still more smoke. "To your knees," he yelled, "and turn down the boardwalk to your right."

They crawled for over five minutes before the smoke began to feather out and surrender some air pockets that allowed them to breathe. Trace stopped, and they all sat on the boardwalk to regroup. Trace looked back just in time to see the roof of the sheriff's office-jail cave in. In moments, the entire building was engulfed in flames.

"Well, I'll be damned if this ain't convenient. Got the whole herd in one place."

A deep voice with a hint of Texas. Trace looked up to see two men not more than ten feet away with pistols pointed at them. One was a big man with a black scraggly beard and a bushy, single eyebrow stretching across his forehead. The other was shorter and chubby-cheeked with a pear-shaped body, who looked more like a chuckwagon cook than gunman.

Bullock said, "Wolf, am I glad to see you, friend."

"Shut up, you stupid bastard. I'm the last thing you're going to see."

"What do you mean? I ain't said a word to nobody. Just let me ride out of here with you, and I'll disappear. Roscoe might've talked, but I ain't."

The two men stepped toward the fire escapees, the man called Wolf aiming his pistol at Bullock's head.

Trace's eyes met Hannah's own. Her shotgun lay on the boardwalk not more than a foot from her hand. He nodded. She understood, he thought, that they were destined for execution killings. They had nothing to lose.

Trace dropped over the edge of the boardwalk and rolled into the street, wincing as pain shot like lightning through his injured shoulder. The big man taken by surprise, got off a wild shot that missed. The shotgun thundered, knocking Wolf off his feet when the buckshot shredded his legs. Trace had his Colt in his hand now and got off two quick shots that burrowed into the shorter man's chest. Trace's target grunted as his legs folded and collapsed beneath him.

He turned his Colt to Wolf and saw the downed man reaching for the gun he had dropped when he went down. But another man appeared from the darkness now and drove a rifle butt into the outlaw's head.

"Friend," the new arrival announced, holding his weapon in one hand off to his side. "This man probably deserves killing, but he might be useful alive."

Trace and Hannah got to their feet, and Trace waved his Colt at his prisoners. "Stay put," he ordered.

A breeze was parting the smoky curtain now, and Trace could make out the face of the other man, who wore what he guessed to be a buffalo hide jacket, which would easily ward off the night's chill. He suddenly had the notion he might like such a coat. Another black beard but a younger man and the whiskers neatly trimmed. The man stepped toward him, first tipping his Plainsman hat to Hannah and then extending his hand to Trace.

As they gripped hands, the stranger said, "My name is Jim Tolliver. Enos Fletcher told me there was going to be some activity I might be interested in near the jail tonight. He even suggested the cobbler's roof would be a perfect place for a good view."

"You're the man who was shooting from there?"

"Yes, I was. Jeb Oaks and his wife were busy from the second floor of the general store next door."

"I can't imagine you were doing this for entertainment. Do you have a stake in this?"

"You could say so. I'm a United States Marshal."

# Chapter 34

DARBY DEFERRED TO Ethan Ramsey for serious examination of Brady Yates's injuries. His years as an Army scout had obviously given him considerable experience with such things. The party had returned to the mineshaft after pulling her and Brady up the canyon wall, agreeing that Brady should be readied for travel back to Lockwood and that it would have been foolhardy to descend the mountain after nightfall.

Brady was stretched out on his old buffalo robe not far from the entrance where they could collect some moonlight. Ramsey knelt over Brady's prone form, probing the injuries. Darby stood behind him holding the lighted candle, which she intended to use sparingly lest it should be needed during the night. Samantha sat near the robe's top, Brady's head settled in her lap, her hand gently caressing his cheek.

Ramsey had found an old tin bucket in the shaft, had washed it out at the stream, and filled it with water to boil on the fire Maddie and Darby had built. He had dipped his kerchief in it and was now washing around the rib wound. "You were right, Darby," he said. "There is not an exit wound. I think the slug is lodged in a rib. It will be painful as the devil if . . . when he regains consciousness, but we'll leave that to Doc Weintraub."

"Do you want me to rewrap it? Maddie said she has a spare shirt."

"Why don't you do that while I look at the leg?"

Ramsey moved to the leg, while Darby worked on the rib wound. The area where the slug had travelled was swollen and bruised, but she saw nothing that would have left the boy in his present condition. It was obvious that loss of blood from the bullet wound had been significant, but after arriving at the mineshaft, Samantha had found a lump hidden beneath his shaggy, unruly hair. "I am shearing that hair down to his scalp when we get home," she had said. "I've been nagging him about it for a month."

There was no sign of a cut on the lump and nothing more she knew of that they could do for it. Samantha had gathered shards of ice from along the stream's edge in a tin cup and was now pressing it against the spot over cushioning furnished by her handkerchief. Ramsey thought the lump might be the real culprit, and Darby knew that the damage they could not see might be the most life-threatening.

Brady moaned while she wrapped his torso, but Darby did not give it much thought. The boy had been doing that off and on ever since she found him.

Then Samantha claimed her attention. "He's awake," Samantha said. "His eyes are open."

Darby looked at the boy's eyes, striking blue. Like Matt Gaines. He looked at her questioningly before looking up at Samantha and giving her a half grin. "Hi, Sammy."

"Hi, Brady." She returned a delighted smile and bent her head and kissed his cheek.

"I need Tag's saddle," Brady said. "I left it behind when I turned him loose and went over the rocks to get to the mine. He followed me here later. But I've got to get the tack. It's worth money. Maybe I can sell it if Butch doesn't try to claim it."

"It's yours, Brady," his friend said without explanation.

Ramsey spoke, "We found the saddle and tack, Brady. I'll get it in the morning before we leave."

Brady stretched his neck and looked down at his lawyer. "Mister Ramsey. What are you doing here?"

Ramsey smiled, "Looking for Trouble. And we sure enough found him. The lady patching your ribs is Darby Crocket, and the young lady next to the fire is Maddie Sanford. They are Pinkerton agents. The wolfdog sitting with Maddie is called Pirate. They came to help."

"I don't understand."

"We'll explain later. Right now, I'm going to be testing your leg. It may hurt some. You just say so if it does."

"Can't hurt any more than my head." He started to drift off again, then opened his eyes. "You won't forget the saddle and tack?"

"Promise. But stay awake till Sammy gives you a drink of water from her canteen. We've got to get you taking in water."

Ramsey turned back to the leg, testing the temporary leather cast and bindings. "I'm not going to tamper with it. You've got that bone bound snug, Darby. I'm afraid I'll just make it worse if I open things up. We'll make a travois tomorrow. I'll cut a few long poles before I ride over to pick up the sorrel's tack. Maybe you and Maddie can work on the rest while I'm gone. Are you familiar with a travois?"

"Yes, I helped put one together for one of our injured agents last summer."

"Good. It won't take us long, and we'll have another use for that rope. We can almost make a mattress out of it."

"How long do you think it will take us to get to Lockwood from here?"

"Hard to say. It will be a lot faster going downslope instead of up, and if this old wagon trail goes all the way to the valley, I'm hoping we can be at Doc Weintraub's by midafternoon. That assumes we can get out of here by ten o'clock or so."

"Well, we've had quite a day. I hope we can snatch a few hours' sleep tonight. I envy my husband. He's probably living a life of luxury at the boarding house."

Ramsey chuckled. "Somebody's got to do it."

# Chapter 35

TRACE, HANNAH, AND Marshal James Tolliver sat in the Ramsey & Locke conference room with a bedraggled and nervous Ferd Bullock. Roscoe Smith and the man identified by Bullock as Wolf Calhoun were handcuffed to beds in separate rooms at the Weintraub Hospital. All prisoners were now in the marshal's official custody, and Jeb Oaks had volunteered to keep watch in the hospital hallway until the marshal made other arrangements for a guard. The dead gunman, who Bullock called Tater Barnes, was resting comfortably at the funeral parlor. None of the meeting participants had enjoyed as much as an hour's sleep the previous night.

Trace had taken some time to clean up and change at Sally's Bed & Board, and the others had done the same at their own lodgings. They had met at The Chowdown for noon dinner before going to the Ramsey office.

Tolliver asked, "Any word on how much damage was done to the bank last night?"

Trace said, "I talked to Matt before I came over here. Not as much damage as the noise and smoke would make you think. It's a stone building, and the dynamite sticks landed in front of the structure. Blew out the windows and started a fire. The Gaines Bank has a new walk-in safe that protected anything of significant value, including bullion and paper money. The windows are being boarded over temporarily. The front part of the bank will need cleaning and painting, maybe replacing of some of the interior wall where flames ate through, but Matt says they'll be open for business tomorrow."

Hannah asked, "What about Craig Hammer. Is he helping at the bank?"

Trace shook his head. "No, he hasn't been seen since yesterday when Matt told him of the former acting sheriff's pending arrest. I am betting that triggered all the chaos, which I confess was more than I ever anticipated."

"I knew he was involved. I just don't know the motive," she said.

Tolliver said, "You asked at dinner how I came to be here, and I ducked the question. When we are finished talking to Mister Bullock here, I will explain. It's time for me to be more forthcoming, so perhaps we can share some information." He looked directly at Bullock. "Mister Bullock, you understand the dilemma you are in, I assume."

"Don't know what that means but know it ain't good."

"Detective Crockett arrested you for suspicion of murder. As a U. S. Marshal, I intend to formalize those charges unless you give me good reason not to. If you don't want your neck in a noose, I recommend you answer truthfully and fully. Of course, if you did kill Sheriff Bridges, nothing's going to save you from the hangman."

"I didn't," Bullock whined. "I swear to God, I didn't."

"Were you present when the sheriff was murdered?"

Silence.

"I asked, were you present?"

"I was, but I didn't know what they was going to do. Honest."

"Who are you talking about? How did you happen to be present?" Trace asked.

Bullock said, "I'll tell you how it all come to be. You see, I was in the back of the cell hall waking up a drunk one day when one of the cowhands—Roy Hill—from the Circle Y come in, and I overheard him telling Will about how he had paid a call on Miss Brisbane, and she begged him to tell the sheriff he had to come out and talk to her. She told Roy it was about the Woods killings."

"Frank and Cora Woods," Hannah said. "Our firm's handling their estates. Ethan is the executor. The ranch and farm ground are going to be sold at auction soon. No family. The will is a public record. The money goes to the Lame Buffalo Association after everything is liquidated and the debts are paid. They were an elderly couple. Murdered in cold blood several months back. Frank was a good friend of Will's, and he took it personally."

"You told somebody, didn't you, Bullock?" Trace asked. "About the message."

"Will took off without saying a word, and I headed to the bank to tell Craig Hammer what I heard. Hammer asked if I knew where Lucy Brisbane lived. I told him I did—not that I ever did go there to visit Lucy, mind you. He said, I should go to The Doll House and see Reggie there. He would have some men to go with me. I told him I didn't want no trouble for Will. My working for Hammer was just a little side job. Deputy's job don't pay shit."

"What did he pay you?" Marshal Tolliver asked.

"Hundred dollars a month in double eagles. Forty-dollar bonus for good information. Got double for this one after it was over. Hell, I didn't get fifty dollars a month for my deputy's job."

Trace said, "So you picked up a few other men at The Doll House and led them out to Lucy Brisbane's to kill her and the sheriff?"

"Like I said, I didn't know what they was going to do. When we got close to the place, I tried to turn back. I didn't want the sheriff to see me there. But they wouldn't let me. I think now they wanted me in on it, so I'd have no way out. And that's the way I felt about it after that. No choice. I was stuck."

The marshal asked, "So what's your story? Who did the killing? Who was at the Brisbane house with you?"

"There was Tater. That's the man you kilt last night. And then old Wolf Calhoun. You got him over at Doc Weintraub's. Sheriff was in the house but must have heard us ride up and came out on the porch. Fired me on the spot. Told the others they was under arrest. Can you believe that? Slick had went into the back way of the house to see to the woman, and pretty soon, Lucy started yelling and Slick cussing. I can still hear her screams from in there, and after a time, a gunshot. Slick killed Lucy. That was just on him. Nobody else touched her."

"And what about the sheriff?" Tolliver asked. "What did he do when he heard the screams?"

"Well, he pulls his Colt and turns back toward the door. Wolf puts a bullet in his back. Will swings around to fire back, and Tater gives him one in the chest. He stumbles off the porch and falls over the steps. Thought he was dead, and we just waited there for Slick to finish whatever he was doing. They was going to set fire to the place. Then, what happens but old Will comes back to life and starts worming toward his gun again. That's when Wolf and Tater filled him plumb full of lead. Slick comes out about then and adds a slug or two of his own."

Trace asked, "What was Slick's last name?"

"Don't know. Only met him that day. Not a man to make small talk with."

"Did he dress any special way?" Trace asked.

"Black. Everything black. Even his gun belt and holsters. But they was all jeweled up."

Trace asked, "Did you see the body I brought in night before last?"

"Nope. By this time, I was minding my own business, and nobody was asking me about anything. When the Pinkertons showed up, I knew I was in soupy shit. I never knew about the marshal here snooping around till he showed up last night."

Tolliver said, "By my count, I'm missing one. You said there were five of you. I come up with four."

"I didn't know the other man. Nobody mentioned his name, and he looked at me like he didn't see nobody.

Didn't do no shooting I could see. But I thought I saw him nod before Wolf started taking down Will."

"What did this man look like?" Trace asked.

"Man gone soft. Tie and fancy duds. Rode well enough, but I'd bet his workdays was usually in an office. Smoked fancy, little cigars he pulled from his coat pocket. Barbered gray hair below the hat brim. Didn't see the top of his head. Thin gray moustache, too. But not old. Not fifty yet, I'd say."

"Tall, short? Fat, skinny?" Hannah asked.

"Just an average sort, I guess you'd say. Kind of in between all that."

Ferd Bullock underwent questioning for another half hour, but the interrogators learned nothing of value.

Trace said, "I do have one question. This man who took Miss Brisbane's message to the sheriff . . . Roy Hill?"

"Yeah."

"Where would I find him if I wanted to talk with him."

"Heaven or hell. Take your pick."

"He's dead?"

"Don't know for a fact. He disappeared the day after Will was kilt. Horse went back to the ranch. A man don't walk far in this country."

Marshal Tolliver said, "Trace, if you and Hannah don't have more questions, I'm going to take this man back to

Jeb's root cellar at the store. If you would just wait here a spell, I won't be gone long."

"Don't like dark, closed-in places like that," Bullock whined, "and I'm afeared there's snakes down there."

Tolliver did not reply and took the man by the arm and escorted him out the conference room door.

# Chapter 36

TRACE AND HANNAH looked at each other across the table after Tolliver left with his prisoner. "You've got something eating at you," Trace said.

"I mentioned to Darby that when I was checking county land records, I ran across several transactions where my former fiancée, Craig Hammer, had purchased parcels of land. They were not farmable and only marginal grazing properties but combined they took up some space, probably more than six thousand acres."

"I don't understand what you are getting at."

"For one thing, Craig doesn't have enough money of his own to swing that. He obviously could not go through the Gaines Bank, the only bank in Lockwood, so it would be outside money. But what really strikes me is that the land adjoined two sides of the land owned by Frank and Cora Woods, the murdered couple. It sits between the

Woods land and mountain country. It merges into the foothills. The Woods estate owns about four thousand acres, good grazing land, Ethan says, and nice farm ground as its east side gets nearer the river bottom."

"But what would be so valuable about that property?"

Hannah said, "The only thing pushing land prices some is the Union Pacific bringing track to Lockwood in the next year or two, but that will run along the west side of the river's course pretty much, and the right-of-way has already been acquired without a fuss. The railroad will benefit everybody—farmers, ranchers, business folks and," she smiled, "even law wranglers."

"The land you are talking about isn't a part of the projected right-of-way though?" Trace asked.

"No. As I recall, a strip on the east end of the Woods tract abuts designated right-of-way."

"Interesting."

"What do you mean?"

Trace said, "That would provide access to a spur across all tracts. I wonder if there have been other parcels change hands out that way."

"I can check the land records, but it doesn't make sense. It would be a track to nowhere."

Trace shrugged. "It's worth looking at."

"I will block out my afternoon tomorrow and see what I can find at the recorder's office."

When Marshal Tolliver returned, Trace and Hannah told him about their conversation.

"It could all be related to why I was assigned here," Tolliver said.

"Maybe it's time you told us," Trace said.

"I was sent here by the U. S. Marshal's office after an inquiry by Sheriff Bridges to inquire about somebody at the Department of the Interior. He had informed the Cheyenne office that it related to unsolved murders in the Lockwood area."

"It was all very vague, but since the inquiry was being made about somebody with a government agency, the top dogs thought the case should be given some priority, and the case was tossed to me. I did some tracking through Interior Department contacts and then arrived here about two weeks ago. The next day, I asked Enos Fletcher to deliver a message to the sheriff to meet me at the livery. Enos was my contact here. He and my dad fought under General Taylor together during the Mexican-American war."

Trace said, "Enos knew about you? That old gossip?"

"I guarantee you Enos is a discreet gossip. More often than not, there is a motive behind the information he passes on. He is more listener than talker. Anyway, the sheriff came to the livery to meet with me, and after I showed him my credentials and Enos verified my good breeding, Bridges told me all he knew. He said the Woodses had been visited on three occasions over the three months before they were murdered concerning sale of their land. During that time, someone kept cutting wire on his fences and driving cattle out at nights. Some of his herd grazing open range on leased government land just disappeared. Not much profit margin in the cow business, and the situation was starting to cause some financial stress."

Hannah asked, "Who wanted to buy the land?"

"Craig Hammer made the first visit, claiming it was on his own behalf," Tolliver said.

Hannah said, "He purchased two adjacent parcels, so that makes sense."

Trace said, "Sounds suspicious to me. From what you've said, Hannah, Hammer doesn't have that kind of money. I'm betting he was somebody else's strawman. That was probably the case on the other land purchases, too." He looked at Tolliver. "But you said there were two more visits."

"The next two were made by a man introducing himself as an agent for Mountain Springs Land Company.

He said his name was Geoff Sparkman, but he was lying. I will explain shortly. Their first meeting was amicable enough until the agent mentioned the rustling that was going on in the valley that was making it hard for ranchers to make ends meet. Frank had checked with neighbors and learned he was the only one dealing with rustlers."

Trace said, "The rustlers must have been some of what the man called Slick called the 'Laramie Riders.' Somebody has had a small army of outlaws holed up to handle jobs to help get whatever they are after. We need to ask our prisoners more about that."

Tolliver continued, "Anyway, the last time this man came by the Woods place, his threats were less veiled. He outright said things were going to get serious soon if they did not sell. Not an outright threat, but Woods went to the sheriff to bring Bridges up to date. A few days later, Frank and Cora Woods were dead."

Hannah said, "You told us this man, Geoff Sparkman, was lying about his name. How do you know that?"

"Frank Woods remembered the man from ten years earlier. He went to an auction for government leases at the Lockwood town hall. A man from the government was auctioning five-year leases on valley parcels still owned by the government. You could lease a whole darn mountain for a dollar back then, Bridges told me. What you would do with it was something else. But I guess some of the leases of grazing land in the foothills and along the valley's fringe could get into serious dollars. Anyhow, that's how Frank got his first lease on some land next to his."

Trace wanted Tolliver to get to the point. "Was Geoff Sparkman there?"

"Yep. He was conducting the auction. All that Woods could remember was that his last name was 'Sharps'—as in the rifle. It stuck in his head. That was the sheriff's only clue at that time, so after the killings, he contacted the U. S. Marshal's office in Cheyenne and asked them to inquire about a man named Sharps with the Interior Department. Not a common name, so easy enough to track. Turns out that Mister Gilroy Sharps has advanced some. He is the director of land management for the Department of the Interior. The land management office handles sales and leases of government lands under jurisdiction of the Interior Department which make up most of Wyoming Territory."

Trace said, "That's a start. But that doesn't explain why Sharps would have any interest in purchasing privately owned land in the valley . . . or have somebody killed to get it."

"No, but there has got to be a connection."

Trace said, "I want to know about Mountain Springs Land Company. I am going to send a wire to the Pinkerton home office in Chicago. Somebody in the Pinkerton network can track the outfit if there is such a firm."

A rapping at the conference room door interrupted the discussion. "It's okay. Come in," Hannah said.

An attractive Sioux woman, probably a year or two shy of her twentieth birthday, Trace guessed, stepped into the room and spoke to Hannah. "Sorry to disturb you, Miss Locke, but I was bringing the papers you wanted back from the courthouse, and I thought you would like to know about the ruckus out on Main Street."

"What are you talking about, Katy?"

"Trouble's coming. Trouble Yates. And Mister Ramsey and the detective ladies are with him. And Sammy Morris. Folks are flocking to the streets. Some are even clapping and cheering."

# Chapter 37

DARBY RODE AT the head of the procession, leading Tag, the sorrel gelding, with the travois trailing behind carrying Brady Yates, who was wrapped like a mummy in blankets and the buffalo robe. Samantha walked beside the travois with her hand firmly gripped in Brady's. Maddie, astride her mare and followed by her faithful wolfdog came next and, finally, Ethan Ramsey and his Appaloosa brought up the rear of the parade, Ramsey clutching a lead rope for three horses, each with a body slung over its back.

They headed directly for the hospital, but Darby could hardly believe it when customers and owners of stores that lined the street poured out onto the boardwalks, many waving, others taking up a chant, "Trouble, Trouble." And soon, everyone started clapping when Brady raised a feeble hand of acknowledgement. It was like a grand celebration despite the macabre scene that brought up the rear of the group. Trouble Yates, still a boy, had many friends in this little town.

Darby's heart skipped a beat when they reached the burned-out jail. Trace. Was he all right? Then she saw him walking briskly toward her with Hannah Locke and a black-bearded man she did not recognize. From the opposite side of the street, she caught sight of Matthew Gaines racing in her direction. When he neared, he darted past Darby and went directly to the travois. Darby tossed a look back and saw that the banker was leaning over the travois as he walked, his sad eyes surveying his son. Samantha, on the opposite side, appeared to be explaining Brady's situation and reassuring the banker that the boy would survive.

When the man she loved reached her, she stretched out her hand, and Trace took it while she leaned over and brushed his lips with hers. "Hi, handsome cowboy," she said. "I'm betting you've got some stories to tell."

He stepped back and grinned, "I'm betting you've got a few of your own."

"Right now, we've got to get Brady down the street to Doctor Weintraub's. Sammy's nursing him along just fine, but he's got a broken leg and a bullet wound in his side that need attention."

Tolliver followed along, but Hannah Locke returned to her office, as they headed for the hospital another block down the street. Trace said, "Darb, the gentleman beside me is U. S. Marshal Jim Toliver. He is working with us now."

"Hello, Marshal. Thank God, we have some real law in this town now." She reached back into her saddlebags and pulled out a coal chunk and tossed it to Tolliver. "Keep it," she said. "I have several others and there are plenty more where that came from. Think about it."

"Coal," Tolliver said.

She saw Trace and the Marshal exchange meaningful looks. "What?" she asked.

"We will talk later, Darb. I see Doc and Nurse Ruth waiting outside their offices. We'd better get the boy situated."

Tolliver said, "Somebody better tell the boy's mother. Their place isn't far from town. I'll ride out and let her know Brady's been found and will be all right. I'll see if I can bring her in."

Darby looked at the marshal just before he turned away to head for the stable. "You are acquainted with Missus Yates?"

"I interviewed her once after the boy disappeared. Nice lady."

"She must have made an impression," Darby said to Trace as he walked beside her mount on the way to the hospital.

"I only spoke with her briefly after I took that bullet in the hills above her house. She was friendly and help-ful. Very pretty, too. But, of course, being married to the most beautiful woman in the world, I don't give much notice to such things."

"Of course, you don't. And you did dance your way out of your comments very adroitly."

Doctor Weintraub hurried toward the party as they approached, and Darby reined in while the physician gave Brady a cursory examination. Nurse Ruth had re-turned to the hospital and reemerged now bearing a stretcher.

Weintraub said, "We can't get your travois through the hospital door, so we'll have to shift Brady to a stretcher." He looked at Gaines who remained at Brady's side. "Matt, I'll need your help. Trace, you stand back. We don't need more damage to that shoulder."

Maddie dismounted. "I can help."

Ramsey weaved the big Appaloosa and his silent fol-lowers through the clusters of people and animals in the street, all giving him space when they saw his cargo. "We will talk later," he called to Darby as he went by. "I will make tentative arrangements with the undertaker. We can all meet at my office later. After supper? Eight o'clock?"

"Plan on it," she yelled back.

Darby dismounted and handed her mount's reins to Trace. "I'll help with moving the patient. Could you lead the horses to the livery after we get Brady onto the stretcher?"

"Yes, ma'am. Anything else, ma'am?"

She scolded herself. She knew he did not like being left out of the action because of his injury. And he liked less taking orders. "I was just asking. If you come back here when you are done, Maddie and I should be free, and we can talk about supper and baths for the ladies."

He grinned. "So that isn't just horses I smell?"

"Likely not. By the way, is that a new coat you are wearing?"

He pretended he did not hear her and began collecting the horses, catching up the reins of Maddie's, as well. He did look quite dashing in the coat, she thought, exuding masculinity. She would tell him that eventually but not before she teased him about the money it must have cost.

# Chapter 38

SARAH YATES WAS standing on the porch talking to Samantha's father, Caleb Morris, when she saw a man driving a one-horse buggy up the river road. Morris had been helping with the cat and livestock chores during the absence of Brady and Samantha. He was a good, hard-working man, reliably calm and quiet in contrast to Millie, his more excitable half-blood Sioux wife. But they were a matched team on the road through life, she thought. She occasionally could not help but envy the pair, but she knew from experience that there were worse things than not having a man. In fact, there were often compensations to being a single woman.

"Do you recognize the man in the carriage?" Morris asked, following her eyes as she watched the buggy's approach.

"I think so. He could be the man who stopped by the night Brady disappeared. Remember, he was here when you brought Samantha over? He asked me a lot of questions. Claimed to be a cowhand looking for work. He said he knew my late husband. But he got me to do all the talking. I remember his speech patterns were strange. Sometimes he slipped into language that sounded quite refined. Other times he sounded like—I don't mean this in a snobbish way—an unschooled old cowboy."

"I understand," Morris said. "And I don't take no offense." He laughed.

She could feel her face heat up with a blush, but she loved Caleb Morris's sense of humor. "I am just saying he wasn't a very good actor. He was something other than he claimed to be, but I don't think he meant me any harm."

As Tolliver reined the buggy into the yard, he gave a friendly wave. "He doesn't look very dangerous right now," Morris said in a near whisper.

Tolliver climbed down from the carriage, tying the black gelding to the hitching post in the yard. He removed his hat as he walked up to the porch. "Missus Yates, I am here to tell you they have found Brady, and he is going to be fine."

"Oh, thank God," she said, starting to tremble. She stepped over to the bench near the door and sat down.

Tolliver turned to Morris, "And, Mister Morris, your daughter, Samantha, with nary a scratch, is in Lockwood looking after Brady while Doctor Weintraub patches him up a bit."

"Doctor Weintraub?" Sarah said. "But you told me Brady is fine."

"I said 'going to be' to cut off your worries right away."

He placed one foot on the first porch step, clutched the handrail and looked up at her with those gentle brown eyes and told her what little he knew about Brady's injuries. "I rented this horse and carriage at the livery with the notion you might like to ride into town with me and see Brady for yourself, maybe pack a few things for overnight and take a room at the hotel or boardinghouse."

She hesitated. She barely knew this man, and she did not want to cause a scandal.

Tolliver evidently recognized her uneasiness and reached into the inner pocket of his buckskin coat and pulled out a leather case, opened it, and handed it up to Morris, who looked at the badge and showed it to Sarah. "I'm not an outlaw," Tolliver said. "I would be escorting you as a U. S. Marshal doing my duty."

"But that night you came to the house, you said. . ."

"A white lie, ma'am. I will explain."

"Well, yes. I would like to go with you. Give me ten minutes." She turned to Morris. "Caleb, we were finished with tonight's chores, but I probably won't be back by early morning. Maybe you wanted to see Sammy."

Morris gave a crooked smile. "I'll see to chores if you will see to Sammy. I need time to figure out how I'm going to give her the news I was telling you about."

"I can't tell Brady right now. Not till he's home."

Morris said, "Sammy should tell Brady."

As the buggy bounced down the rocky road to Lockwood, Sarah cast a glance at the sturdy man holding the reins beside her. His beard made him seem older at a casual glance, she thought, but she guessed now that he was short of forty, not a lot older than her thirty-four. It seemed strange to sit next to a man in a carriage after so many years alone, but there was something comfortable about the closeness that she did not mind a bit.

"You are sure Brady will be okay?"

"As sure as I can be, ma'am. He was on a travois, and he was conscious. There were too many others around, so I couldn't get in for a close look. And that gal was watching him like a hawk, shooing away anybody that got too close."

"Please, call me 'Sarah.' Ma'am makes me feel old."

"I will do that. But remember, when we met, I said I was James."

"James it is. Not Jim?"

"Most call me Jim, but I let special folks call me James. Maybe you wouldn't mind?"

"No, not at all. I think James has a more distinguished ring to it."

Tolliver laughed. "Distinguished. Now I've never been called that by anybody. Speaking of names, I noticed your son goes by different names. Some call him Brady, and others tag him Trouble. There must be a story there."

"Yes. Just a little thing, but the name stuck." She told him about the school teacher and Butch Hugel.

"It's funny, how one little incident will trigger a nickname that sticks for life," he said. "Happens all the time."

"He's fine with it. He answers to both. Some folks jump back and forth. One day he's Brady. Another day he's Trouble. To Sammy and me, he's always Brady."

"He and Sammy must really be special to each other."

"They are. Practically raised together. Same age. Living just across the river from each other. And she's always been such a tomboy. I can't remember when they weren't best friends. But now they're getting to an age where things are going to be different. Sad, in a way. Touchy, if you are a parent. They never had rules between them, but we've had to start paying a little more attention to their time together. But I think they are aware, too, possibly just trying to deny something is happening. Maybe it's a good time for the change that's coming."

She had expected James to inquire about the change, but he remained silent, leaving it to her to decide whether further explanation was due. She liked that. "Caleb and Millie Morris are selling the quarter section where their house is located and moving back to Iowa to take over his father's farm."

"A sudden thing?"

"A surprise to me and their kids. The UP railroad acquired an option on the property over a year ago, Caleb told me, for the track they are planning to build on the other side of the river to connect to Lockwood. It will be several years before the line is finished, but it will provide a connection to Cheyenne and Laramie and three or four other towns."

"The end for stagecoach travel out here," Tolliver commented.

"But new opportunities for the town. I might even open a shop again. The lady who took my old place over couldn't make it pay and closed up. I own the building and rent it out for storage now. I could hire help and teach others, sew when my hands were working, but mostly manage and handle the business side. Brady is always talking about things he wants to do when the railroad connects. He's an ambitious young man. I would like to have a project of my own again.

Tolliver said, "Sounds like he got some of that ambition from mom."

"I have some things to think about, but it's time for me to get off my fanny and stop wallowing in self-pity."

"I have a hunch you are overstating your behavior, but I think it is good for folks to stretch themselves some, keep their brains and bodies moving as much as their strength allows." He hesitated, "I've got my marshal's hat on now. Tell me, had Caleb Morris been expecting the option to be exercised this soon? Do you know?"

She replied, "Now that you ask, he did say that the option ran for another two years. He was expecting to farm the land at least one more year before he got the notice. He wasn't even sure the purchase would ever be finalized. That's why he and Millie never said anything to the kids. Brady told me once that the track would go through the Morris place. Matt Gaines had sketched the logical route when they were talking at the bank. Brady just thought the Morris family would put up a new house and farmstead on the quarter section they owned west of their present home."

When they reached town, Tolliver took the carriage to the hospital and left Sarah there after checking on Brady's condition. He promised to come back about suppertime and see if she might be able to get away to join him for a quick supper. He also volunteered to make lodging arrangements for her at the Lockwood Inn, where he was staying.

Sarah asked, "Would you ask if they have a room with an extra bed in case Sammy needs a place to stay? I do appreciate this. Nurse Ruth says I can see Brady in a few minutes, and this saves me a lot of hassle."

"I am happy to be useful. Why don't you see if Samantha would like to join us for supper if she hasn't made other arrangements?"

Sarah thought the gesture kind, but she would not have minded dining alone with this man.

# Chapter 39

TRACE, DARBY, AND Maddie dined at Sally's Bed & Board after the women had completed bathing and changing into the dresses that they had worn the first day in town. Sally had volunteered to arrange for the laundress next door to wash and dry the riding garments and underthings. Hanging before a big fireplace, they would be ready by morning if the wearers did not mind a smoky scent, Sally had assured them. Pirate, bursting with scraps and leftovers, snoozed contentedly in the corner of the dining room.

They had arrived late for supper, and the five other guests had excused themselves from the table, leaving the privacy they were hoping for. Ample portions of roast beef, mashed potatoes and gravy remained. Trace took a small helping of broccoli to be polite and stirred it around with his fork until Darby kindly stole it from his plate a sprig at a time. Good woman. She always had his back. He had the good sense, however, to keep his slice of cherry pie out of her reach.

They had already exchanged summaries of their adventures since parting less than two days earlier. Now, they hoped to put their conclusions together before meeting with the marshal and others at the Ramsey & Locke offices in less than an hour. Trace welcomed cooperation with Marshal Jim Tolliver and any others with a shared interest, but they needed to remember they were Pinkerton agents and responsible first to their client, Matthew Gaines.

While Sally removed the plates and silverware from the table, they continued to talk. Trace said, "Those few lumps of coal you brought back from the mountains. Do you think this is the missing link—what the sheriff's murder was all about?"

Darby said, "Ethan told me that if there is a real strike up there, it could be bigger than gold. The demand is growing like wildfire with no end in sight. Mining is a hard, tough business, but the labor is easy enough to find. Transportation is the key. You must get it to the users. A lot of them are back east, and there are producers in Pennsylvania and West Virginia, but settlement is growing west of the Mississippi, and the west coast is becoming a huge coal market. Wyoming Territory is positioned to cash in on it. There have already been some finds northeast of here."

Trace said, "And the Interior Department is on the verge of selling the source of the coal at auction for pennies of what it's worth."

"And Mountain Springs Land Company is waiting to pick it up," Darby added.

"Hopefully, we will hear something from the home office tomorrow about the Mountain Springs outfit. In the meantime, Jim has sent a message to his superiors recommending that the Secretary of the Interior be advised to freeze all land sales in Wyoming Territory pending completion of the investigation. Jim's information was that the sale date is still at least a few weeks off. There are notice procedures that cannot be bypassed. The problem with government sales is that most enterprises ignore them unless they have inside information. I suspect that the insider here is the property manager, and he expects to end up as the owner of the coal mining land. It wouldn't take much capital investment once he owned the land. He could lease it out to mining outfits and become a multimillionaire on royalties without putting out another nickel."

"Speaking of the marshal," Darby said, "I understand Sammy joined him and Sarah Yates for supper at The Chowdown."

Maddie said, "Yeah, she's going to stay with Missus Yates at the hotel tonight. I'll bet the marshal wishes she would stay someplace else."

Darby looked at Maddie with narrowed eyes. "Maddie, why on earth would you say such a thing?"

"I saw the way he looked at her when he dropped her off at Doc Weintraub's office. I know a horny man when I see one. He didn't have marshal business on his mind."

Darby said, "This conversation has taken a crude turn. What would you know about such things, anyway?"

Maddie grinned, "More than you might think."

Trace did not doubt her one bit. He had not been with Darby for a good spell now. He was not about to let Maddie get a good look at his eyes.

# Chapter 40

THE LAW OFFICE meeting included the lawyers and the Pinkerton detectives, as well as Marshal Tolliver and Matthew Gaines. They gathered at the long table in the Ramsey-Locke conference room, so the group deferred to the senior partner to preside.

Ramsey directed his first remark to Gaines. "How is the boy doing, Matt?"

Gaines said, "I stopped by the hospital on my way here. The slug's been removed from his rib and the wound stitched. The leg is set and splinted. He said you folks did a good job stabilizing the break when you were up the mountain."

"That was Doctor Darby Crockett's work," Ramsey said.

"The splinting was nothing compared to being dragged up the side of that canyon," Darby said. She wondered if her back and butt would ever be the same.

Tolliver said, "Sarah's mood was almost bubbly when I left her and Sammy after supper. They were going back to the hospital for a quick visit with Brady. He needs a good night's rest, and then I think a few of us can speak with him in the morning."

Sarah, now? Darby was not so certain that Brady's condition was the sole cause of Sarah Yates's uplifted mood. "We need to locate Craig Hammer. He is obviously connected to this in a major way." She turned to Gaines. "Have you seen him, Matt?"

"No. If he had no part in this, he would have returned to the bank today to help with cleanup. He lives in a little rental house a few blocks off Main Street. I went over there late morning and knocked on the door. No answer. I don't know where he would be. I can give you directions. You'll want to check again."

Trace asked, "Do you think he could have saddled up and ridden out of town?"

Gaines rubbed his chin. "That's what puzzles me. He doesn't own a horse. He came to town on the stage, and he travels horseback only when necessary to visit a bank customer. You could check with Enos Fletcher and see if he rented a mount there. Gaston's Stable is nearer Hammer's house, so you would want to ask there, too. But I just don't know how he would go far on a horse. I suppose he could follow the stage road, so he wouldn't get lost. Otherwise, he wouldn't stand a chance out in the wild. He's a city boy through and through. I don't know how in blazes he ended up here."

Darby said, "He must have had some references. You said he's been here about two years, where did he work before?"

"Oh, my God." It was Hannah.

"What is it?" Darby asked.

"He worked with the Department of the Interior in Washington. He talked about his friends in Washington all the time. He was an accountant there. Do you think he was part of a plan when he came here?"

Trace said, "Somebody didn't dream this up overnight. I'm betting he and Gilroy Sharps have known each other a while."

"I remember now," Gaines said. "His references did come from the Interior Department. Files like that probably got eaten up in the fire, but I'll look. I just wonder if one of his reference letters didn't come from the director of land management." He sighed and shook his head in disbelief. "This has been going on right under my nose. I should have smelled a rat."

Ramsey said, "You couldn't have known. Nobody around here was aware of coal deposits in the mountains. Somebody suspected, likely Sharps, and had it investigated. He has probably been checking out prospects at other places under his jurisdiction as well—which would include most of the territory. Of course, the coal was nearly worthless except for a limited local market until the railroad became reality. This has been a long-term project for a man in a position of influence and power."

Trace asked, "When does the stage south come in next?"

Gaines said, "Stage to Cheyenne leaves late tomorrow morning. Same route you came in on. Lockwood is a turnaround stop. You're not thinking Hammer would be foolish enough to try to board the stage here?"

Trace shrugged. "I suppose not."

Darby could tell Trace was up to something. But what? "Do you have something in mind?" she asked.

He winked. "Nothing I'd want to talk about in mixed company."

The remark elicited a round of nervous laughs, and she could feel her face flush. The clown would pay for this.

Trace continued, "How about tomorrow morning, Maddie and I and the wolfdog see what we can do about tracking down Craig Hammer? Jim, you've got Brady and two prisoners over in the hospital to interview. Maybe you and Darby could talk to them."

Damn him. Trace always had a way of slipping in and taking charge. Maybe it was the ex-West Pointer in him. In her head, she knew it did not matter. Two people who liked to be in charge had gotten hitched. Fortunately, the situation rarely led to confrontation. They gradually carved out their areas of authority, and other times, they did their little dances around each other.

They tossed some more ideas out for discussion, but a half hour of that was plenty.

Later, back in their room at the boardinghouse, Trace undressed for bed while she combed out her long, golden hair. She checked the dressings on Trace's shoulder which Nurse Ruth had re-done before the meeting. Everything appeared to be holding nicely. Trace dropped naked into bed, while she finished undressing, slowly and seductively with her back to him just to tease a bit.

"I can't believe you are randy after all you've been through," she said, "but if you've got something in mind, I'm game for a quick go. More than game, in fact. We will have to take care of that shoulder. You just lie there and let me do the work." She was also thinking of her sore backside.

Clothes neatly put away, she turned and stepped toward the bed in the dusky lamplight, deliberately trying to arouse him further. She slid beneath the sheets and snuggled up to him, nibbling at his ear, placing her fingers on his chest and dragging them down the taut flesh of his abdomen toward his vulnerable place. Strangely, he did not respond. She lifted herself upon her elbow and looked at his face. He was dead asleep, oblivious to her presence. She collapsed back on the bed, vowing to tell him in the morning—after they were up and dressed—about what he had missed out on the night before. Let him squirm all day.

# Chapter 41

TRACE AND MADDIE went to Craig Hammer's house and knocked on the front door. It was a tiny place, but the outside was well cared for, Trace noticed, fresh white paint, even on the privy out back. He knocked again before turning the doorknob and discovering the door was not locked. He opened the door and stepped in.

"Aren't you supposed to have a warrant or something to do that?" Maddie asked from behind him.

"Where did you get that fool notion?"

"I think I learned about it at school when we studied the Constitution."

"You've got to consider these things in the context of the situation."

"Darby said to be careful of you, that you say nonsensical things sometimes to avoid giving a straight answer."

"We don't have time for straight answers at the moment." He walked around the parlor, as Maddie and Pirate followed him in. Spartan furnishings. A cowhide settee and matching stuffed chair. A large fireplace took up half of one wall, and there was a bookcase on each side, both with plenty of empty spaces. He plucked out one of the books and examined it. *Coal: Man's Ride to the Future.* He thumbed through some of the other titles and found most were about the coal industry, several about mining techniques. It appeared the young man intended to be a "hands on" executive in the coal business.

A kitchen separated by a half partition was just off the parlor, and an open door led to a small bedroom. If Craig Hammer did not plan to return, he had left a lot of wardrobe behind. Checking the closet, Trace found several nice suits and expensive shoes. The man had good taste, he thought, but Trace was a boots man.

They wasted no more time in the house. They stopped at the Gaston Stable on the chance Hammer might have rented a horse there. Orval Gaston was a plump, doughy man who didn't bother to get off the bench in front of the stable. A quick glance at the horses in the corral told Trace that the animals had seen better days. They didn't appear starved, just old and worn down. Gaston was an unpleasant man, and Trace could see why the rundown place did not do much business. Gaston told Trace that he had never heard of Craig Hammer, which Trace considered unlikely in a small town, but he decided not to press further until he talked with Enos Fletcher. He could always come back. He hit a gold mine at Fletcher's Livery.

"Yep," Enos said. "I thought somebody might be asking. The weasel come by here last night. Wanted to rent a horse and said he needed it saddled and ready to ride before sunrise. He looked like hell. Think he'd been sleeping on a haystack. Starting to smell some. Not the Mister Fancy Pants that a feller saw at the shiny desk outside Matt's office at the bank."

"How long did he want to rent it for?" Trace asked.

"Two days, he claimed. 'Course he needed saddle and tack. Ain't sat a real saddle much, I'd guess. Probably just one of them pimples they call saddles back east. He didn't have no cash money. Give me a bank draft for rent and deposit. Think it's any good?"

"I don't know. You might want to run it to the bank real fast. So he has been here and left with the horse?"

"Yep. I rented him Five Mile."

"Five Mile? That's the horse's name?"

"Yep. Tired old gelding. More pet than rent horse. Some like to rent him cause he's gentle as a sleepy lap cat."

"Why do you call him Five Mile?"

"Thought you'd never ask. He's not good for more than five miles."

"What do you mean?"

"He just stops after five miles. Won't go no further. Rider tries to beat him, and that horse turns into a bucking bronco. There's still life in that old cuss. Once he throws the rider, he just turns around and moseys home. I gave him Five Mile, because I knowed that weasel had no intent of bringing my horse and tack back."

Maddie said, "He headed down the stage road, didn't he?"

"Yep. I'm guessing he was going to get out of town and catch the stage to Cheyenne down the road someplace. Man like that couldn't make it to Cheyenne on the best horse. And he was traveling light. No grub or nothing. He stuffed a flour sack in his saddlebags, and the rattle wasn't flour. I'm betting it was gold bullion and other cash money he could have given a poor old stableman." He chuckled. "If he made the mistake of whopping Five Mile, the weasel won't be taking the saddlebags with him."

Trace pulled out his pocket watch. "Stage could be coming anytime, we'd better move."

Enos said, "Get your horses out. I'll trust you for rent and deposit. A little something later for the information wouldn't be turned away."

"You've got it, Enos," Trace said as he hurried to the back of the stable to retrieve his favorite horse.

In less than fifteen minutes, Trace and Maddie, trailed by the wolfdog were headed down the stage road, moving their mounts at an easy lope. Trace led an extra baldface mare. Enos had been waiting at the stable door when they were ready to take their mounts out. "You will likely need an extra horse," he had said.

The old devil was always a step ahead of him, it seemed. A man had to take care not to underestimate Enos Fletcher.

"Keep an eye to our backs, Maddie," he called. "If we see the stage coming down the trail, we've got to flag it down. Tell them not to take on another passenger."

Shortly, they saw a riderless, iron gray horse coming their direction, stopping to graze as it suited the critter. "That's got to be Five Mile," Maddie said.

"Yeah, that's our guy."

The horse did not spook when they came near, just looked up from his grazing and eyed them curiously. "Should we take him with us?" Maddie asked.

"Nah. At least not now. We can pick him up on the way back if he's not already back at the livery. Looks like he got away with the saddlebags."

They continued on, and a half hour later came upon a young man dressed in a crumpled business suit sitting by the stagecoach trail, knees raised, arms folded over his knees and face buried in his arms. They slowed their mounts to a walk, and as they neared the man, he seemed unaware of their presence.

Maddie spoke barely above a whisper, "He's shaking like a leaf. I think he's crying."

They dismounted some twenty feet away and Trace warned, "He's probably armed, so get your Winchester out and ready."

When she had her rifle out and in firing position, they stepped forward. "Craig Hammer?" Trace said.

The young man looked up. His eyes were red and swollen, and tears streaked his dust-caked face. Blood streamed down the left side of his head, probably the result of his vault from the saddle, Trace figured.

Trace said, "We're Pinkerton agents, Mister Hammer. We've come to take you back to Lockwood. We hope you will come peaceably. I think you have a gun. If so, please hand it over."

"I know who you are. My Derringer is inside my coat. I'll take it out and hand it to you."

"Just toss it on the ground."

"Certainly." He reached under his coat and eased the gun out, and suddenly turned the barrel toward himself, pressing it upward under his chin.

"No," Trace yelled, "don't." He lunged to wrest the weapon from Hammer's hand.

The gun fired, a mere pop compared to some larger weapons, but lethal, nonetheless. Maddie shrieked. Blood erupted instantly from the hole the slug had bored. Still, Hammer sat there for several moments, his eyes glazing over, before he toppled forward and lay twisted on the ground.

Maddie turned away. Trace understood. She had seen blood, dealt death herself. But it was not the same as watching a man in what should have been his prime years take his own life.

Later, as they tied Craig Hammer's body to the spare mount, Maddie said, "I wonder how Hannah's going to take this."

"They were history," Trace said. "She broke up with him."

"I loved a bad man. He was killed, and most would say he deserved it. But I still think of him and cry for him sometimes. Because someone is history does not mean they never existed and weren't important to you at one time."

Trace thought about what she said. "You are a wise young woman, Maddie Sanford."

# Chapter 42

DARBY AND MARSHAL Tolliver sat down in chairs set in front of the bed in Brady's room at the Weintraub hospital. Brady sat up in bed with his back propped against pillows, and his mother sat off to one side and Samantha on the other. Brady had insisted that his friend be permitted to stay, and Sarah agreed.

Tolliver had suggested that Darby lead the questioning, suggesting that the boy might be less intimidated by a female questioner. Darby was glad to do it but thought the marshal had much to learn about Trouble Yates.

Darby said, "Brady, I understand you will probably get to go home tomorrow."

He looked at her with those piercing blue eyes as if telling her to get to the point. "Yeah," he said, "Mom's going back to the house this afternoon and taking Sammy home, too. She's coming back in tomorrow for some kind of business, and she said the marshal here will help her get me home after she's done. What did you want to ask me?"

"You weren't in condition to talk when we were up in the mountains, but you ran away from home. We think you saw something. Did you?"

"Yes. I saw some men kill Sheriff Bridges, and then some of the killers saw me in the trees."

"How did you happen to be there?"

"I went near the house because I heard a woman's screams and then a gunshot. Then, after a bit there were other shots." He went on to explain how he happened to be on the trail and what he saw when the sheriff was shot in front of the house.

Darby said, "There were five men then?"

"That counts the one in black who came out of the house just before I ran."

"Did you recognize any of the men?"

"The deputy, Ferd Bullock."

"Did you see him fire his gun at the sheriff?"

"No, ma'am. I'm sure it was holstered. But he wasn't doing anything to stop it. I thought that was strange."

"You didn't recognize any others?"

"Well, there was another guy all gussied up in a suit and tie that seemed out of place. I'd seen him around town maybe three or four times over the past two years. I've been thinking about that. The last I remember seeing him was in early summer. He was coming out of The Chowdown with Mister Hammer from the bank. They were talking and laughing like old friends. I recall this fella slapping Mister Hammer on the back. Figured he was some out-of-town banker the Gaines Bank worked with. Mister Hammer would know his name."

"Was he Mister Hammer's age? An old school friend maybe?"

"Oh, no. A lot older. Not old enough to be his father or anything, but he had gray in his dark hair below his hat. Never saw him without his hat."

Darby said, "We need to find out who has been coming in and out on the stage here the past month. I gather the general store acts as agency for the stage line. That's where we got off when we came in."

Sarah said, "Jeb and She Bear act as Wells Fargo agents. Not enough business for a fulltime agency here."

Tolliver said, "We need to talk to either Jeb or She Bear about this man that Brady saw. You're thinking he could still be in Lockwood."

"A possibility, anyway. If Trace finds Craig Hammer, we might get some answers from that source. He seems to have been the local contact. In the meantime, we can't let today's stage pull out without checking the passengers."

"I will keep an eye on the stage if you want to talk to Jeb or She Bear Oaks."

Darby turned back to the boy. "Brady, I would like to have you do something for us. If you agree, I will ask Nurse Ruth to bring in a wheelchair and I will roll you down the hall and have you peek into the other two rooms. In each room there is a man handcuffed to a bed. I want you to tell me if you recognize either of them."

"Sure, I can do that."

The nurse brought in a wood-framed wheelchair with two leg supports that could be raised separately or together. Nurse Ruth and Sarah helped Brady into the chair lifting the injured leg, wrapped in a Plaster of Paris cast, onto one of the raised supports.

Tolliver asked Darby, "Would you like me to roll Brady down the hall?"

Brady was already manipulating the wheels on the big, high backed chair. "I'll do it," he said and headed for the door.

Darby feared he was going to crash, but he zipped through the doorway with an inch to spare and turned

sharply down the hallway. Darby and Tolliver followed. He paused at the first doorway and eased partway through the opening to Roscoe Smith's room and studied the man who slept there. Without comment, he backed out and rolled to the next room. There, he rolled further into the room. Darby stepped up behind him and saw that Brady and Wolf Calhoun were engaged in a stare-down of sorts. It appeared that the man with long, tangled hair and scraggly beard was trying to threaten the boy with his angry glare, but Brady was unflinching.

"Let's go, Brady," she said softly. He reluctantly backed away.

Back in Brady's room, the boy rendered his verdict quickly. "The second man, the one who looks like his name, was there. He was one of the shooters. He likes killing, I think. I hope I can take time off work to watch him hang. I've never seen a hanging."

His words, so matter of fact, took Darby aback for a moment. What a strange boy. "You would testify in a courtroom that he was one of the killers, then?"

"Sure. The young guy, I saw once going into The Doll House. I was outside selling a kitten to two of the whores. They said they needed a ratter, but I'll bet he got spoiled rotten and didn't turn into much of one."

# Chapter 43

TOLLIVER AND DARBY met on the charred board-walk outside the former jail. "I spoke with both Jeb and She Bear," Darby said. "They have a ledger with names of all stagecoach passengers who have come in on the stage or embarked for the last two years. We're welcome to look."

Tolliver said, "I watched the stage pull out fifteen minutes ago. Nobody remotely close to the guy we're looking for. Of course, with a bit of money he could board the stage some distance down the road. Or he could have hired an escort and left on horseback."

"Enos would have told us if a stranger had rented a horse."

"The mystery man obviously has contacts who would furnish a horse."

Darby said, "Jeb said the guy he suspects we are looking for came in on the stage a week before we arrived and hasn't left, with Wells Fargo anyway. He has taken the stagecoach in and out of Lockwood every three or four months for the past two years. He can supply dates from the company ledgers. The man is usually in Lockwood a week but sometimes two."

"Did Jeb give you a name?"

"Geoff Sparkman. He always stays at The Doll House."

"Interesting. I didn't know they lodged long term guests."

Darby said, "Think about it, Jim. Geoff Sparkman. Gilroy Sharps."

"I'm missing something, I guess. Oh, I see. Same initials. And it fits with what Will Bridges turned up from Frank Woods. You think the big fish himself might be around here?"

Darby shrugged. "Somebody at Pinkerton told me that more than half the people who use fictitious names pick something with the same initials. Keeps you from getting tripped up on personal things that have your initials written on them or maybe something that's been engraved or etched."

"Makes a certain sense."

"Well, if Trace brings Craig Hammer in, maybe we can confirm that."

The marshal said, "Speaking of the devil. I think that's Trace and Maddie coming from Fletcher's Livery."

Darby looked north down Main Street and could make out Trace and Maddie riding abreast, Pirate trailing not far behind. What caught her attention, however, was the horse Trace led with a burden slung across its back. As they neared, she confirmed it was a body.

"Looks like they found Hammer," Tolliver said.

"We needed him alive. He could have been a great help. And it's terrible. We're piling up bodies like it's a war. Jeb rented one of his warehouses to George Caldwell to store corpses. He was going to refuse to take them until Matt Gaines guaranteed payment. We might put several burials on the Pinkerton expense account. But this many?"

"Did you say Jeb rented a warehouse to the undertaker? I hope it's not the one Matt said the county would lease for a temporary jail. I can't leave Bullock in the root cellar forever, and soon the two prisoners should be moved from the hospital. We've found two laid off cowhands to work twelve-hour shifts as guards, but I need to get the jailbirds under one roof."

Trace and Maddie shared grim looks when they reined their mounts up to the boardwalk. Trace had saddlebags slung over his good shoulder and slid the load to the crook of his arm. "Marshal," he said, "Enos asked me to give this to you. Craig Hammer was taking this with him. I took the liberty of shuffling around in the pockets. One's full of a fair amount of cash. The other's got copies of telegrams and correspondence between him and Gilroy Sharps, some on Interior Department letterhead. I'm thinking the gentleman was holding an insurance policy or blackmail cards, maybe both if he got tossed to the wolves."

Tolliver reached up and took the saddlebags. "Maybe you folks will help me sort through this later. I guess I'll see if I can get it in the bank safe for now."

Darby said, "It appears Wolf Calhoun and Roscoe Smith are about all we've got left. Maybe we could stop at The Chowdown and have a sandwich, Jim, and then visit the hospital again. If you can catch up, Trace, you and Maddie can join us for a quick lunch."

"We're not going to starve, but after we see the undertaker, the horses need to go back to the livery. We'll find you someplace."

Darby said, "Ask Enos if he has ever heard of Geoff Sparkman or Gilroy Sharps."

# Chapter 44

SARAH YATES GOT up from Brady's bedside, satisfied he was sleeping soundly. She spoke in a near whisper to Samantha across the bed. "I have that appointment with the lawyer at one o'clock. When I'm finished, I'll come back, and we can pick up the carriage and take you home. I know your parents must be crazed with worry."

She left, nervous about the task ahead but convinced she could not even think of picking up a new life until she faced up to the horror that had haunted her for over four years. She realized now that the burden had been wearing her down more than the accursed disease, possibly aggravating her ailment.

When she exited the Weintraub offices, she encountered James and Darby. They exchanged brief and perfunctory greetings, but she could sense that James was worried about her. It was rather nice to have a man worry about you. Alfred had for about two months following their marriage. Matt had during their interlude, and she thought might have since but had been in no position to express concern.

Thankfully, Ethan Ramsey did not keep her waiting, and she was shown to his office before she even had a chance to take a seat in the waiting area. He greeted her, quickly putting her at ease—or as much as she could be under the circumstances. Ramsey came around the desk and turned one of the client chairs so it was facing her and sat down. His secretary appeared with two cups of coffee before they got past Ramsey's inquiries about Brady's condition.

That done, the lawyer asked, "How can I help you, Sarah?"

"This is very difficult, but I have something on my mind. I must face it. Consequences be damned."

"I'm listening."

"If I told you I committed a crime, what is your obligation as a lawyer?"

"First, if you say you are going to commit a crime in the future, I have a duty to report to authorities. Now, if you are charged with a crime and you confess to me, I am still entitled to defend you, plead you innocent and force the prosecutor to prove you guilty beyond a reasonable doubt. I would not let you testify in that case. Finally, if the authorities have no knowledge of a crime, my responsibility is somewhat murkier, but I am thinking I must report it for investigation."

"I see." She thought she understood. She desperately wanted to clear this up, but an investigation would get complicated. Brady would be questioned.

Ramsey sipped at his coffee. "I have an idea. Why don't you just tell me a hypothetical story. Pretend it is fiction. Tell me a story about someone else. Keep it very brief, as few details as possible."

"I guess I can try. It starts out this way. This woman's husband beat her, and she had a very unhappy marriage. He left for long periods and then would return from time to time. Finally, one day he disappeared, and it looked like he might never return. She hoped not. But they owned a farm, and after five or six years, a lawyer assisted her with a court procedure to have the husband declared dead, so she could inherit the farm."

"Okay. The woman has committed no crime to this point," Ramsey observed.

"But after that the husband returns. He wants the farm sold, so he can take the money and leave. He says it is his money." She hesitated. "He says he knows their child is not his. He strikes the child several times and throws the child to the corner of the room. Then, he beats her, nearly kills her. She pulls his gun from its holster. It drops on the floor, and he continues pommeling her. She reaches for the gun, grabs it, shoots him in the chest, and, for good measure, places another shot in his head."

"A terrible experience for the woman," Ramsey says. "Did she call the law?"

"She panicked. She was afraid her son would be taken from her. After she had rested, she dragged the body to the horse lot and buried him there, only a few feet deep. But she knew the livestock would bury him deeper in manure over time. That's what she thought he deserved then."

"Interesting case," Ramsey said. "The lady killed a man who was already dead. I don't suppose a prosecutor or jury would buy that notion, though. I can tell you this: I cannot imagine a prosecutor filing a complaint in a case like this. I doubt that a crime was committed. Self-defense first comes to mind."

"There is another possible complication. There is a man the woman likes and considers a special friend. There is not romance, but if there should be more, she could not have this lie between them. And he is a U. S. Marshal. He also claimed to know the woman's husband when they first met, but he was vague as to how that came to be."

"Sarah, if you speak with this lady, put her mind at rest. She would never be convicted in such a case. It may not even be necessary to bring this to light. Let sleeping dogs lie, one might say. I must think about this. I also think the woman's lawyer should make a discreet inquiry of the marshal about his connection to the woman's twice-deceased husband. I think there is something missing here, a piece that the lady has not divulged, but that's okay. Tell the woman there is nothing to worry about. Her lawyer will be in touch soon."

When they prepared to leave Lockwood, Samantha offered to drive the carriage to Sarah's place and said she would put up the horse before she took the footbridge across the river narrows to the Morris home. They bounced down the road slowly, savoring a balmy day, for they would be home well before dark. This girl was like a daughter to her and tears came to her eyes when she thought a time was approaching when she would not see Sammy almost every day. And Brady, how would he react to the loss of his dearest friend?

"Sarah," Samantha said, as she slowed to negotiate the buggy over a washout, taking care that the dapple gray mare did not catch her hoof in the hole, "you seem very sad. I hope the lawyer didn't give you bad news."

"No. No. I'm just dealing with some personal things about Brady's father."

Samantha said, "Brady's told me some things, swore me to never tell, and I would die first. But you already know. You were there. I feel funny talking about it, but I've told Brady he should discuss it with you."

Sarah felt her heart racing, pounding, ready to leap from her breast. "What did he tell you?"

"That he killed Alfred Yates and helped bury him in the horse lot. I can't help but think about it whenever I go in there, wondering if I am stepping on his grave. Brady thinks maybe his bones should be dug up and moved to someplace else, but he says you have never talked about it since that day. You told him you killed your husband, and he should believe that and say that if anything ever came up. You saying you killed your husband did not make him believe it, and I think you know that. He was only nine years old, but he remembers every detail. And he would never, never let you take the blame."

"I know. I just want to put this behind us somehow. It's a ghost that haunts me, probably Brady, too."

Samantha said, "Probably Brady not so much. He has a way of putting things behind him, sort of closes a chapter and can't wait to get to the next one."

"I suppose you are right."

"There is something else. I doubt if he would ever say anything, but you should know."

"Yes?"

"He knows that Alfred is not his real father. He heard your husband say that several times that night. He did not hear you deny it. And he is glad Alfred is not his father. He will never ask you this, but in the worst way, he would like to know. If it would hurt the other person, he would never approach him. He would just like to know. I hope I haven't hurt you by saying these things."

"No, Sammy. You have given me much to think about, but your words will help me make the right decisions about some things when the time is right."

# Chapter 45

TOLLIVER ASKED TO lead off with questioning the two prisoners who were technically in his custody at the hospital. He and Darby sat in Roscoe Smith's room talking with the young would-be gunslinger. He was much improved, Darby thought. He would recover quickly, although he could not replace his right trigger finger. He would learn to shoot a firearm with the other hand, she assumed. She hoped he would reconsider his choice of careers.

"Smith," Tolliver said, "tomorrow you get moved to a new jail we're setting up. So far, you haven't been tied to any killings. If that holds and you help us out, I will drop the charges and turn you loose in a few days. It is in your hands."

"I want to go home, back to my dad's farm in Nebraska. It looks better there every day. I left because of the quarreling with my dad all the time. I'm thinking maybe he knew more than I gave him credit for. He can't handle all the work. Maybe my ma will help us make peace. I'll tell you what I know, but it ain't much."

"How long have you been here, Smith . . . in the Laramie River Valley?" Tolliver asked.

"About a month, a little more. There was about ten of us come here as a crew. About that many more started early spring, I guess."

"What did these crews do?" Darby asked.

"Whatever we was assigned. There was seven or eight hard-nosed hired guns—like Slick and Wolf and Tater. Others of us would be drafted into gun duty when needed. Sometimes, we just watched folks to report what they was up to, like out there where that wolf tried to kill me. I was just going to relieve Slick that night and then saw these other folks and didn't know what to do. Damn wolfdog settled everything. Sometimes we watched the mountain trails. Foreman—I guess that's what you would call him—said to report to him if we saw anybody heading up in the mountains with digging tools."

"Did you ever see anybody?" Darby asked.

"I didn't, but some did, and I guess the hard noses were called in to deal with it. Don't know what they did about it. Didn't want to know."

Tolliver asked, "Where did you headquarter?"

"We stayed at a ranch out north and west. Somebody said the paymaster owned it."

"Paymaster?" Darby said.

"Yeah. He come out Saturdays and paid us in cash or bullion. Didn't have to cash no drafts or nothing."

"Who was the paymaster?" Darby asked.

"Somebody at the bank, I heard. Hammer. That was his name. Hammer. He was the money guy."

Tolliver asked, "Who was the foreman?"

"Oh, that was Reggie Weaver. The Doll House guy. All the orders come from him. Good guy. Once a week, we could do shifts and visit his girls. Not his best, but they was friendly, if you know what I mean. Of course, it weren't free. Got what he called a discount, though."

"Did you know anybody higher up than Weaver or Hammer?" Darby asked.

"Nope. Don't know that there was. Don't know what the hell it was all about, to tell the truth. Just drew my pay, and half the time didn't have no work to do. Told us we was just waiting in case something came up. Like with that kid everybody was looking for. Trouble, they called him. Don't know why they wanted him. They put me on watch at his ma's house, so I didn't go to the mountains."

They asked five or six more questions and decided there was nothing more to be learned from young Smith. Darby felt they were putting more pieces together, however.

When they were settled in Wolf Calhoun's room, the marshal commenced the questioning again. "The doctor tells me he can probably save your legs and that someday you should be able to walk to the gallows with a cane."

The man's hostile scowl faded, and Darby could see the marshal had grabbed the prisoner's full attention.

"Hanging. I didn't do nothing to take me to a noose," Wolf said.

"You killed a lawman. That's the fastest way to the noose. You are a dead man, mister, and you won't need those gimpy legs to swing from a rope. Not in hell, either," Tolliver added. "Now we've got an eyewitness, two if you count former deputy Bullock. You don't think he's going to speak up to save his own neck?"

Darby could see the fear creeping into Wolf Calhoun's eyes. Tolliver knew his job.

Tolliver continued. "I can't promise you anything. I don't have authority to make any deals, and I don't think you are a candidate for one. If you help, I will tell the prosecutors. You know as well as I do that nobody's going to come around to help you. For your information, the paymaster, Craig Hammer, is dead. Do you want the others to walk away free as birds while you take full blame?"

"Ask your damn questions."

"Who did you take your orders from?"

"Reggie Weaver at The Doll House."

"There was a man present at the sheriff's killing. He wore a suit. Who was he?"

"Don't know. Reggie called him Geoff. Seen him at The Doll House twice before, but never talked to him. He always sat at a table near the back, where him and Reggie talked. Thought he was just a friend of Reggie's till he went with us that day. Then I figured out he was something more, like maybe somebody calling shots for whatever we was doing all the shooting and running around for."

"Why was he with you?"

"I gathered he wanted to see for his self that the sheriff and the whore was dead. He didn't talk much, but he kept calling her 'Lucy' like he knowed her good. He'd been poking her. I could tell that."

Of course, Darby thought. Pillow talk. Geoff Sparkman, also known as Gilroy Sharps, said something that suggested to Lucy Brisbane he had been somehow involved in the murders of the ranch couple. Bragged maybe about what a big man he was going to be and how folks were learning not to get in his way. Some drinks could have loosened his tongue, so he spilled out even more. She was probably a gunman's target and had figured that out. That is why she sent for Will Bridges.

Darby said, "You told us you saw Geoff at The Doll House several times. Is it possible he stayed there when he was in town?"

"I suppose so. Seems odd he'd go to see another whore, if he had one in the next room ripe and ready." He grinned, revealing broken, rotting teeth. "Of course, some men got peckers that's always looking for something different. And some of The Doll House ladies ain't the cleanest."

A man of Gilroy Sharps's stature might take more care than some, Darby figured, and likely sought out safer companionship.

Tolliver turned to Darby. "Are you thinking what I'm thinking?"

"Yes. If you are thinking we should gather up Trace and Maddie and head for The Doll House."

# Chapter 46

THE MARSHAL AND detectives gathered at Fletcher's Livery, which provided a direct view of the side street on which The Doll House was located. It was early afternoon yet, so Trace figured there would be few in either bar or brothel.

For purposes of working out the logistics of their approach, Trace asked Enos Fletcher if he knew anything about the physical arrangements of the place.

"Like I say, I never been in there. A real man—pardon me, ladies—don't pay for such pleasures."

Trace tried to erase the images of the women who might be seduced by Enos Fletcher. He had heard it said there was someone for everybody, though. "I just thought you might have had a drink there or something, the place being so close by."

"Hell, no. I don't go to my competition."

"How do they compete with you?"

"They've got their own stable out back. Can't see it from here. Customers that don't want to be seen can stable their horses there, go in the back, take care of their business and be on their ways. Don't got to pay poor old Enos a darned nickel."

Now, Trace knew the real reason for Enos's dislike for the place. "So, we'll need to cover the back entry. Maddie, can you and Pirate take that? Your wolfdog doesn't need to eat everybody that comes out. Just have the double-barreled ready and hold them in place."

"We'll do our best. All they got to do is cooperate."

"I think either Jim or I should go in first. A man wouldn't draw as much attention as a woman. I'll go, if it's okay with you, Jim."

"I represent the law. I'm thinking I should do it."

Trace dug in his pocket and pulled out a coin. "Heads, I win. Tails, you lose."

"You don't really think I'm falling for that?"

"Slip of the tongue. Heads, I win. Tails, you win."

He tossed the coin and it landed at his feet. The men both knelt to examine the coin. "Heads," Trace said, snatching up the coin.

Tolliver's hand locked on his wrist. "I want to see the coin," he said.

Trace opened his hand and Tolliver plucked out the coin and stood. The marshal turned the coin over twice as he examined it. "I thought so. Double heads. Oh, hell, if you want the job that bad, you can have it."

Trace saw Darby staring daggers at him, but he did not reject Tolliver's concession. "Well, let's get about our business."

As they walked down the boardwalk and neared The Doll House, Maddie peeled off and, followed by her wolfdog, trotted along the side of the huge barn-shaped structure toward the rear of the building. Trace noticed as they neared the double-doored front entrance that the building needed paint, the clapboard front having washed down to nearly gray, bare boards. The long sign that stretched along the front was similarly fading into its background. The doors, on the other hand, were thick, sturdy oak, and were more challenge than he would admit to muscle open with his single working arm.

He stepped inside, stunned for a moment by the contrast. A virtual palace with crystal chandeliers, walls decorated with paintings of life-size or larger naked women, a few of male and female entwined in contorted positions. It wouldn't take long to make a sale once the customer got through the door, he figured. And no peeling or washed-out paint inside.

Tolliver and Darby slipped in behind him, each moving to separate sides of the entryway, backs to the wall. Trace started a casual walk toward the ornate bar that covered half the width of a room that stretched a good seventy-five feet, he estimated. Only two men stood at the bar, but they wore sidearms low on the hip. They appeared to be ignoring his presence, but they were men to keep an eye on. A man with a rifle cradled in his arms stood at the top of a winding staircase. It was a good bet that the bartender at the far end of the bar, who watched him with interest, had a weapon within reach.

Then he caught sight of the man off to his right sitting alone at a table positioned at the inside corner of the room, his back to the wall, of course, facing the door. This would be the boss's table. Trace guessed him to be in his late thirties, too young for Mister Sharps. Long black hair was pulled back in a ponytail, and his face was decorated with heavy eyebrows and moustache. He sipped at a drink while keeping his eyes fastened on Trace. Two more men sat at a table some ten feet distant, and Trace doubted they were customers.

He supposed the back entrance/exit was behind the wall that backdropped the bar. Another less grand stairway, for both escape and privacy, probably funneled to the same outlet.

He turned to the man in the corner and took several steps in his direction.

"Stop right there, Mister Crockett. State your business," the man said evenly.

"Since you know my name, I guess we don't require introduction. I'm guessing you are Mister Reggie Weaver. According to a telegram I received this morning, you are vice-president of Mountain Springs Land Company, second in command to the president, Mister Geoff Sparkman, also known outside the public filings as Gilroy Sharps.

"Must be a mistake on the records some place. Never heard of such an outfit."

"We would like to speak with you and make a search of the premises. The man at the door is a U. S. Marshal."

"Got a warrant?"

"You know the nearest judge is in Cheyenne," Trace said. "The marshal is here in pursuit."

Weaver smiled. "In pursuit of what?"

Trace said, "In pursuit of Gilroy Sharps and Reggie Weaver."

"Go to hell."

Those words must have been a signal, because the barroom exploded with gunfire. Trace fought off the temptation to check his back and focused on the men in front of him. Weaver remained in place, but the two at the other table started to stand reaching for their pistols. Trace took one down with a gut shot before the man cleared leather. He dropped to the floor, dodging a bullet from the other before he raised his Colt upward and drove a slug in the gunfighter's chest.

"Don't be a fool," he yelled, as Weaver stood and tried to search out Trace between the tables with his own pistol. Weaver seemed to recognize the futility of his situation and placed his weapon on the table.

It occurred to Trace that the room was silent, and he stood and turned around, relieved to find his wife and friend still standing not that far from their positions at the entrance.

"The man at the top of the stairs was going to take you out," Darby said. "Jim nailed him, but that started the fireworks."

Trace looked about the room. The would-be assassin lay head down on the stairway. The bartender stood behind the bar with his hands in the air. The men who had been standing at the bar were on the floor, one writhing and moaning and the other showing no sign of life.

The distinctive roar of a shotgun sounded from the rear of the building, and Trace crashed past the chairs and tables and around the bar, charging through the opening behind it. The door was directly ahead, and he drew his Colt again before pulling the barrier aside. He stepped out cautiously, almost running in to a grinning Maddie.

She nodded toward the ground, where the wolf-dog had a suited man pinned. "I think I caught the big fish," she said. "I just fired the shotgun in the air, so you wouldn't forget about me."

# Chapter 47

SARAH WAS SURPRISED when her lawyer, Ethan Ramsey, appeared at her door. "Ethan, what a surprise. I didn't expect you out here."

"It's a nice morning, and Patch thought it was perfect for a ride. We won't have many more of these till spring. Sometimes lawyers make house calls, and I thought we should talk. Privately. You may come out here, and we can take a short stroll, if you like."

"I am alone," Sarah said. "Sammy came over bareback on her old mare, and somehow Brady climbed aboard, and they went into the foothills to talk." She didn't say how worried she was about the outcome of their outing. "So you just come in. I've got a fresh pot of coffee that doesn't even need warming."

Ramsey sat down at the kitchen table, and she poured two cups of coffee before she joined him. She waited expectantly.

"Brady is apparently doing well, if he can go for a ride," Ramsey said.

"I can't slow him down. He moves faster on crutches than I can walk on my best days. I don't think he is all that upset by things he has experienced. They're just past adventures to him. He's always looking ahead."

"He truly is an exceptional young man." He hesitated. "I had just as well get to the subject I came to discuss. I assume you heard about the ruckus at The Doll House three days ago."

"Yes. Caleb Morris was in town, and he told me about it. He thinks the newspaper will be doing a big write up on it, and he will bring me a copy."

"Well, all of this has kept Marshal Tolliver pretty busy, and I didn't have a chance to talk with him until yesterday afternoon. Sarah, your husband, Alfred, was a wanted man. We don't have to talk about this hypothetically anymore. He killed two women. You don't want to know the worst of it. There was a 'dead or alive' reward on his head. You would have received a thousand dollars if you had reported the killing. I know you would not have wanted it. Jim was after him as a lawman. The trail turned cold in Cheyenne, probably about the time Alfred showed up here. I think somehow Brady did the killing and that is why you didn't contact the law. Am I wrong?"

"No."

"Here's what I am advising you to do, Sarah. Show me about where Alfred is buried in the lot. Give me permission to tell Matt Gaines about it. In the spring, you find an excuse for you and Brady to go to Cheyenne for a few days. Matt and I will come out and dig up Alfred's remains and take them up in the mountains and bury them next to Butch Hugel. If Brady wants to know where, I'll tell him. But you need the remains off this place to close the chapter."

"You would really do this?"

"Of course. And since it's not lawyer work, it won't cost you a nickel." He took another sip out of his coffee cup, leaving it half full, and stood to leave.

"I just don't know how to thank you, Ethan," she said, following him to the door. He turned to her and smiled. "None needed. I'm sort of like Brady Yates, I guess. We both like our adventures."

She watched from the doorway as he mounted the big Appaloosa and started to wave, then stopped. "I almost forgot to tell you about Jim Tolliver. I haven't told him why I asked about Alfred. What you say to him or when is up to you. But in case you are interested, when this case is tied up, he's resigning the marshal's service and staying in Lockwood. He has been offered the sheriff's job, so I suspect you will be seeing him around town on occasion."

Ramsey tipped his hat and nudged the gelding toward the river road.

# Chapter 48

"WHY WOULD YOUR father want to leave the valley?" Brady asked. "I'd never leave. Ever. I know you don't want to go." He was on the verge of tears at the news Sammy would be moving.

They sat face to face on their favorite stones in the hills above the river. Both leaned forward, their heads almost touching, as they spoke in soft voices as if trying to keep their conversation a secret from the world.

Samantha said, "I had a terrible fit. I threatened to run away. I asked if I could stay with you and your mom. I said I would hate Iowa and that I would make them miserable there. My mother said she and I would talk the next day, and we did. She explained that my grandfather was ailing and that he owned a half section that would go to my father when grandpa died. And he's alone. Dad's

two brothers are both dead, killed in the war. We're needed there."

"Bring your grandpa here."

"We're near to losing the land here, Mom said. Dad's
more farmer than rancher. We settled here because Mom
had relatives, but they've moved on or died. Some went
to the reservation in South Dakota. I never knew about
the money troubles. Mom didn't either. Dad kept it to
himself. And I don't really want to be away from my family—my parents, or even my brothers, as bratty as they
can be."

"But what about us? We've always been best friends."

She looked up at the same time, and her chocolate
brown eyes met his blue ones. He saw the tears stream-
ing down her cheeks and suddenly realized his selfish-
ness. "We can write," he said. "Just Nebraska between
Iowa and the territory. We'll have a train soon right into
Lockwood. It will just be a quick jump back and forth. I'll
come visit you. And you can come out here, maybe stay
with ma and me for a whole summer."

Samantha said, "You have good intentions. But you
won't write. You're always into some new project. You will
be too busy. Don't make a promise you can't keep. But we
can try it. I'll write, but if you don't answer, I won't write

forever. We're not leaving till April. Dad may go on ahead because he has to be in Iowa for planting."

"What about the quarter section the railroad's not buying?"

"We will keep that for a spell. The railroad money for the home place will let Dad pay off the debts here. Your mom is going to manage the other parcel and rent it out with your land for now. Dad thought you might want to add it to your place sometime."

"I will. I can keep a part of you here that way. And you will come back to see it. You're a mountain girl. I know you will."

# Chapter 49

THE DETECTIVES HAD their belongings loaded on the Cheyenne stage and would be boarding and pulling out to commence the grueling journey shortly. They had said their good-byes to the marshal, soon-to-be sheriff, earlier. Their client, Matt Gaines, was there to see them off, and Darby was surprised when she saw Hannah Locke rushing across the street.

She was nearly breathless when she reached them. "I've got to run," Hannah said. "Judge came to town with the stage, and I've got a hearing to squeeze in before Judge Halsey takes on all the business you've left for him."

Darby said, "We truly thank you, Hannah, for all you've done for us. I wish we had gotten to know each other better under different circumstances."

"We can get together again. I am writing my father. I plan to make an extended visit to the Flint Hills in June.

We'll get together then if you are not on an assignment someplace."

"That would be wonderful."

"I am committed to return to Lockwood, but it's time to see my father and my brothers. Ethan and I have agreed to a month's leave from the firm." She hugged Maddie and then Trace and Darby, whispering in Darby's ear, "Too bad he's taken." She hurried down the street past the bank toward the town square and the stone courthouse.

"What did she say?" Trace asked.

"That you are the ugliest man she ever met."

"I don't think so. Not in this buffalo hide coat I'm wearing."

"We still need to talk about that coat."

Gaines had stood back while Hannah said her good-byes, and now he moved in close, shaking hands with each detective and thanking them. "The fees will be in your Kansas bank when you arrive in Manhattan, including bonuses. I will leave it to you to cut out your share and send the balance to Pinkerton."

"He won't like that," Darby said. "He doesn't like anybody to know what his share is."

"More than he deserves, I'm sure. Anyway, I am just grateful Brady is back safe. Sarah has said she would like for him to spend more time with me. Says she wants to meet with me and my wife together to talk about the boy soon. I don't know what she's got in mind, but Martha and I will help her and Brady however we can." He gave a wry smile. "They are quite a self-sufficient pair, though. I don't think they will need my financial help."

Trace said, "You and Brady have already established the groundwork for a friendship. From here on, it's just going to be extra special. And I'm betting someday he pulls you into a business deal."

Later, as the stagecoach rolled down the natural path carved through the mountains, Darby remarked, "A lot of happy endings back there."

"Yeah," Trace said, "I'll be happy if we beat that snow Jeb said was headed this way."

Fortunately, they had the coach to themselves because other prospective passengers had forgone the trip due to concern that a major snowstorm might block a return trip for days, if not weeks. Maddie had a seat across from Trace and Darby. Pirate had his own ticket but chose to ride on top of the stage for now. He would bark if he wanted to claim his seat.

"Speaking of happy endings," Maddie said. "What happens to me when we get back to Manhattan? Do I get a detective job?"

Darby said, "Trace and I have been talking about that. You have more than earned it. If your father would agree to it, what would you say about moving in with us?"

"Live with you?" She beamed. "I would love it. I know I would. Pirate would, too, out on your ranch. We're ranch kids, you know."

"You would have to obey our rules."

Maddie hesitated. "I would try."

Darby supposed that was the most they would get out of the girl for now. "You would have to attend high school. We would arrange for someone to stay with you if a detective assignment would interfere with your education."

"I guess I can do that."

"Finally, we would work out a visitation arrangement with your father. You could take the train to Kansas City to visit him periodically. And, of course, he must agree to all of this."

"He will. He knows he can't keep me and Pirate there if he forces us to go back. We'll walk in one door and out the other."

Darby said, "I will talk to our lawyer when we get back to Manhattan. Some type of guardianship papers will need to be drawn up."

"Another happy ending," Maddie said, her satisfied smile betraying her feeling of a battle won.

Or the beginning of a nightmare featuring this wild girl-woman and her wolfdog, Darby thought.